THE LONG SHADOW

GAYNOR GABRIEL

authorHOUSE®

AuthorHouse™ UK Ltd.
1663 Liberty Drive
Bloomington, IN 47403 USA
www.authorhouse.co.uk
Phone: 0800.197.4150

© 2013 by Gaynor Gabriel. All rights reserved.

No part of this book may be reproduced, stored in a retrieval system, or transmitted by any means without the written permission of the author.

Published by AuthorHouse   11/27/2013

ISBN: 978-1-4817-9724-5 (sc)
ISBN: 978-1-4817-9723-8 (hc)
ISBN: 978-1-4817-9725-2 (e)

Any people depicted in stock imagery provided by Thinkstock are models, and such images are being used for illustrative purposes only.
Certain stock imagery © Thinkstock.

This book is printed on acid-free paper.

Because of the dynamic nature of the Internet, any web addresses or links contained in this book may have changed since publication and may no longer be valid. The views expressed in this work are solely those of the author and do not necessarily reflect the views of the publisher, and the publisher hereby disclaims any responsibility for them.

Contents

Chapter 1 1
Chapter 2 15
Chapter 3 23
Chapter 4 27
Chapter 5 37
Chapter 6 51
Chapter 7 67
Chapter 8 77
Chapter 9 97
Chapter 10 109
Chapter 11 123
Chapter 12 137
Chapter 13 145
Chapter 14 155
Chapter 15 161
Chapter 16 167
Chapter 17 171
Chapter 18 179

For my children and grandchildren, with all my love

Acknowledgement

I would like to thank Sara Maitland who read my novel in its raw form. Her comments and encouragement spurred me on to continue working on it. She is inspiring.

Chapter 1

SOPHIE PURSUED ORDINARINESS WITH A passion. She was the extraordinary daughter of an immigrant Jewish family, fugitives from the Polish pogroms of the end of the nineteenth century. This resolute woman's quest was to blend into drab grey streets, colourless faces and bent shoulders of Cheetham Hill, in the North of Manchester.

Sophie was a baby when she and her parents arrived in the North of England, exhausted, penniless, afraid and speaking no English. Strangeways, Manchester, by the station, was to be their ghetto home for some years to come, a world apart from the homeland they had left behind. For them, the place lived up to its name. Here there were no fields, no gardens, no green, no vistas; row upon row of houses, and mills and smoke. Charcoal burners on street corners drew the many out-of-work men irresistibly like flies to temporary brightness. There had been enough money, contacts and prescience to enable the family to leave their home and make the hazardous journey to safety. In her new milieu Sophie was brought up to be inconspicuous, to fit neatly camouflaged into a new culture, a culture where Jews were part of the fabric. She later bequeathed her handed down fear to her own family, an inheritance through many generations lodging inside ribs like concrete. They were all set on becoming the salt of the earth, no single grain any different from the next; with centuries residing in souls, fear scarcely understood, only known and felt. 'Suffering is the badge of all our tribe' was Sophie's often quoted phrase, a line of least resistance.

Daniel, a small boy, had 'come over' in the same group. Many thousands didn't escape the pogroms and of those who did many didn't survive the hardships of the journey. Those who arrived struggled with extreme poverty which most of them had never known, clutching their few belongings closely to them, not for any value they might have had but for the solace they gave. Sophie and Daniel's families had supported and comforted each other through the trials and heartache of their displacement. On arrival they had been found, through contact with a Jewish network, two upstairs rooms of a mean, unheated terraced house which they shared, four adults and two children. Downstairs was a family of five only too glad to let out their upstairs for a few shillings rent. The two women, Rifka and Ada, mothers of the little Sophie and Daniel, cooked on a small smoky solid fuel stove in the corner of Ada and Karl's bedroom, it being the larger of the two rooms and every evening one of the men brought a bucket of coal upstairs from the dingy cellar. Both rooms were damp, a greeny-black mould growing in swathes on ancient wall paint and flourishing more vigorously in the winter. There was scarcely room to move between bed and small cheap wooden table and chairs. The two families had half an hour very early in the morning to use the sink in the kitchen downstairs for washing, and washing up, in cold water. The whole household shared the privy in the backyard.

The Jewish families had constantly to remind themselves that they still had their lives. The two men, Sophie's father, Ivan, and Daniel's father, Karl, did any work they could find, mostly in the rag trade, humping bales of cloth and machine parts from warehouses to sweat shops, repairing machinery, cutting patterns, fixing and winding bobbins; no task was too menial and no hours too long for a wage that was scarcely enough to feed the family. They observed and listened, picking up skills and language in their squalid and exploitative new milieu. They had been quite comfortably off in the old life, Ivan running his own printing business and Karl owning a small farm. Every day they both thanked God for their lives when they prayed together walking to work. There was not much else to be thankful for. There was little work for the women to do. Rifka, Sophie's mother, found casual work cleaning machinery in a small cotton mill. Ada became depressed, inert, and undernourished. She died quite soon after their arrival in England, from untreated septicaemia. The day his wife died Karl stopped praying, and set about lifting himself and his son Daniel out of their wretchedness. Ivan continued to pray, now mostly for his sins, as he joined his compatriot in lying, copying keys, stealing, working from first light till the arrival of the work force, taking cottons, materials from bales, small enough amounts not to be noticed; using machines, intercepting customers, covering up their tracks, offering cheaper and quicker service and home visits for fittings. The abjectness of the two men inspired their audacity. It worked. They were able, before their sins found them out, to move out of Strangeways to more dignified ways. They each rented small, solid houses in lines of stark, identical terraces fronting onto the street. The families rejoiced inside their palaces. 'If only Ada could have hung on,' was Karl's passionate and daily lament.

After an undistinguished few years at elementary school Daniel and Sophie helped their parents with their small tailoring business in the cramped front rooms of each house. It was the best they could do. The children had had a bad start at school on two counts; the language and their provenance. Their parents never spoke English at home and always had difficulty with the language. They had been urged to keep quiet about their Jewishness, no need to broadcast it since it always appeared to cause problems.

They were so close it seemed almost inevitable that Daniel and Sophie would marry, and they did so at the age of eighteen. They took over Karl's small house and his part of the business when Karl, still grieving for his wife, even after many years, and disillusioned on finding a strong current of anti-semitism in his surroundings, and still struggling with the language, took himself off to try and find solace and solitude in the North East of Scotland. His sadness killed him only two years after his departure.

Daniel and Sophie worked hard with Sophie's parents and kept their heads down. When Ivan and Rifka decided they were too tired to continue the young couple took over and, in its small way, the business flourished. It was not difficult for Daniel to achieve a kind of anonymity, always impeccably polite at the same time as telling the world he liked to keep himself to himself. Being quiet and unobtrusive was more difficult for Sophie. She sparkled with vitality; shiny black hair, dark skin, piercing brown eyes, a bony patrician profile, a small woman with a huge presence and a fiery nature. And she knew like a missionary what would be best for her future family in an alien and blatantly anti-semitic milieu. She crackled with the antithesis of what she strived for.

Fortune smiled on the young couple. Two daughters, Ada and Queenie, grains of salt, easily taken for Gentiles, quick to like grey, navy, black, pin-stripe, but especially grey, were being moulded into spectacular ordinariness. Extreme hardship, both physical and mental, caused the premature deaths of Ivan and Rifka but they died satisfied that they had found a new and better world for their progeny. Queenie followed faithfully in her mother's footsteps, turning an indifferent face to anything within her that slightly suggested success, achievement, difference, later always issuing to her own two children subtle injunctions to please by merging into mediocrity.

Grey-cloth sobriety stemmed urges and carefree fancies. Crouching, eyes downwards, the two daughters trod a dusty-dry edgy path between success and sin. They did well at school in their quiet way and, with no higher expectations, began to acquire their parents' skills at the age of fourteen. Ada did well, except for the end. She died young, from choice. Her previous most audacious act took her out of her parents' sweat-shop home into Beecham's Pill factory where she packed pills for the rest of her short life. Some pills never made it into the glass bottles, finding their way instead into the hem of her overall. Nightly the pills were hidden inside a pincushion. She was intent on leaving the Jewish garment makers, the greyness, unable to find colours in her life, enduring serious depression. She had found it impossible to flourish in the stifling atmosphere at home and the monotonous daily grind at work. Her grandmother had scared her to death when she was a young girl. They were forced to go and visit her nearby, Sophie desperately trying to get her to be part of the family and the community; which she never became. Queenie somehow managed the visits without too much bother but Ada had dreams about this strange old woman whose attempts at English were incomprehensible. She had a witch-like look about her and insisted, every visit, on squeezing both girls very tightly, muttering words in a harsh sounding language over their heads. Ada cried a lot after each visit and continued to be afraid of her grandmother well after Rifka's death. She knew the story of the families' flight and arrival and could not relate to it. It was unreal, nothing to do with her life. And here was this strange woman, supposed to be her grandmother. Her sister Queenie didn't share her unease. They had little in common and rarely played together. Ada felt alone and didn't understand why her mother was over-protective, wouldn't let them go out much with their friends, never let them have birthday parties, told them always to be polite, quiet and obedient. Queenie was good at this way of being which made Ada feel more isolated.

The ambulance, the shame and embarrassment, the tight, cold little funeral, the silent questions, her absence, all were shrouded in grief and impotent anger. Responsibility stabbed at Sophie and Daniel forever. Daniel especially lamented that they had been unable to connect their children with their past whilst trying to ease them into a culture which had been so difficult for his, and Sophie's, parents and his wife. Ada had a distracted air about her as if she was only half listening and half living. Daniel knew that she felt, in her own way, dispossessed as he himself did so often. Such a link never occurred to Sophie. Nothing was said out loud, not a word shared, they continued their fearful pursuit of plainness finding no way to renounce their legacy of persecution. Their second daughter would be a remarkable credit to them they were sure. Of course, Ada had 'died of a heart attack, so tragic, so young, all her life before her'.

In time Queenie sinned splendidly, being pregnant at nineteen, and by a Gentile. Sophie, in spite of her quest, would still have preferred her daughter to marry Jewish. Queenie had been allowed to go out to the pictures every week with her friends Enid and Margaret and it was during the interval when she met Enid's brother, Leonard. It happened soon after, behind the cinema and only once. When she knew, after the second month her period didn't show up, her greatest fear, indeed terror, was telling her mother. She knew of other girls in her predicament who had been sent to homes, institutions for unmarried mothers, had their babies adopted, and some of them stayed in the institution. She knew that the shame of families was so intense that they'd turn their daughters out of the house onto the street. She would never be allowed to stay at home to have the baby let alone hope for some support from her mother. Her dad would comply with her mother's decisions. Would her mother hit her across the face as she had done a few times when she was fiercely angry? Where would she go? Leonard had been shocked by the news and sullen. He couldn't do anything, he'd said. He was only twenty, he'd said, and didn't want a baby. Or a wife. Enid had told her that he'd always been useless.

They were having cottage pie for Sunday lunch. Sophie served it out and Daniel asked, 'What's the problem, Queen? You look down in the dumps.'

'I'm . . .' There was a pause. 'Going to have a baby.'

The parents stopped in their tracks for a few seconds.

'You little tramp!' Sophie shouted. 'Don't you dare tell another soul! And who, might I ask, lady, is the proud father?' Sophie was shaking with rage and shame and had stood up, leaning across the table, pushing her face towards her daughter. Daniel sat silently, elbows on the table and head in hands.

'Well? Speak up madam!'

'It's Leonard, Enid's brother.' Queenie had her head turned away, trying to avoid her mother's outrage.

'Look at me!' Queenie timidly, tearfully turned towards her mother who continued. 'He's not even Jewish. Oy oy oy. And as far as I know he's a layabout. You *stupid* girl. How could you do this to us? What are we going to do with her, Daniel? How come we had such daughters?' She shook with rage.

Queenie took refuge in her bed whilst her parents made plans for her future. She would marry Leonard; he would have no say in it. Sophie knew his mother and knew she would force him to marry Queenie, since he didn't seem to want to. That was the thing to do in these circumstances. And the other thing to do was to get the couple as far away from home as possible. The other side of the city. That way no-one would know.

The wedding was quick, plain and, above all, explainable; 'Leonard would be working on the other side of Manchester. They want to be together, naturally. How we'll miss them, such a lovely couple, he'll be very good for her. We won't see them for a while, such a long journey, two trams and two buses.' Clouds of hot air obscured the rage, the disgust, the humiliation, the near loss of respectability. Everyone knows but no-one lets on, an endless unwinnable game when tight-shut lips and lids cooperate silently. After a daughter, Josie, was born Queenie furtively visited her parents in Cheetham Hill from Lime Street, on the south side of the city, infrequently and alone. Time and the birth of another daughter, Sarah, eased the tensions, a little.

Lime Street, Queenie and Leonard's new home, was a street of small Victorian terraced houses, at a time when small Victorian terraced houses were not fashionable, yet a cut above slums. Their house was dark and cold, except for the living room where a fire, almost always lit, and always small, blazed like a beacon in the middle of a large black-leaded range with an oven either side and a metal plate on a long arm which would swing over the fire when needed to heat up pans and kettles on the hearth. There was always a jam jar full of spills rolled from newspapers for lighting cigarettes next to a hand brush and pan for the ashes. Physical privacy was a luxury the family knew nothing about. As they were growing up the confinedness drove Sarah to create vast spaces and infinite privacy inside her head and body where secret thoughts, dreams and emotions abounded. Josie didn't mind the restraint, even seemed to take comfort in it like being wrapped in a woolly blanket. The parents showed the world a nice, respectable happy front to a cold affectionless marriage.

The family stood out for two reasons; one, having a lime tree in the tiny front garden in a street with no other trees; only privet.

They had privet too, and gladioli. Two, they were the only ones in the street to have a car, a black Austin Seven, an object of great pride to Leonard. He lavished more time on it than he did on his family. He had a firm belief that he was far and away superior to the people in the neighbourhood and this was one way of showing it. He wasn't allowed petrol as the vehicle wasn't 'essential' but he always managed to find some.

Queenie made all the clothes for the two girls, Leonard set type for a newspaper and both neglected to tell their daughters they were Jews. It was wartime and Queenie and Leonard's two daughters walked a mile from Lime Street to Elementary School with gas masks like black dogs strapped to their backs. Catarrh and glasses created a lot of difficulty for Sarah in her gas mask. She could scarcely see anything through the mist on her lenses and could hardly breathe, her lips tight shut to stop the nose-drippings slipping in. She dreaded gas mask parade feeling she was more likely to die from a gas mask than from a German bomb. Josie was pleased to get out of lessons. They had heard talk of evacuating the school but it never happened, unlike the High School which disappeared to Blackpool. Most people preferred to risk the Blitz than the dislocation to faraway places.

Evenings and sometimes whole nights were often to be spent with some of the neighbours in the communal air-raid shelter in the Congregational Church grounds, drinking thermos tea or milk and eating whatever cake turned up, frequently slab cake. The shelters were no protection against a direct hit but offered protection against the flying debris of a near miss. Not everyone came to the shelter. Some had their own steel boxes, Anderson shelters, in the place of now upended settees in front rooms families scarcely used except for high days and holidays, or at the bottom of the garden if one had such a luxury. Some huddled under the stairs in the belief that somehow this cramped dark space was safer than anywhere else in the house. The loud bangs were 'only guns' the children were told, as if to reassure.

The shelter was known to all as The Savoy. Billy, the next door neighbour's son, smiled vacantly through the noises. His 'Nana' was always there first to secure their places furthest away from the Elsan toilet. He was not quite right they said though not in front of his no-nonsense grandmother. Sarah's family never had much to do with them. Billy's dad had walked out on his mother who was not all she should be. She had never set foot inside the air-raid shelter. Mrs. Morrison always came into the shelter with Hayden, her small puny boy, and a bucket. Hayden was invariably sick in air-raids, a creamy slow sick, not the throwing up kind, and out of his nose too. They all sipped their tea and ate cake with the rank smell in their noses of Hayden's vomit and the Elsan behind a curtain. Mr. Mottram sat in his usual place by the door and defiantly smoked Woodbines one after the other in spite of the large poster on the wall above his head saying Smoking Prohibited. Jessie, Queenie's best friend, only friend, blond and waspish, sat entwined with her little ginger haired daughter, potentially waspish, in a blue and grey checked blanket.

Even in the shelter habits developed quickly, sources of comfort in a mad world, a need for predictability. The elderly Mr. and Mrs. Boot sat in their deck chairs, glad of a change of scene and company. Mrs. Sidebotham and her blond children, Mr S being 'away at the war', bemoaned the fate of the world. 'What's it all coming to?' like a chorus at every verse end, in this case at every lull, accompanied by a slow shaking of the head. 'Widow Twanky', (Mrs. Thomson), 'I never go out without me warpaint on, bombs or not,' always present and correct. May and Ernest with their little white(ish) Yorkshire terrier which was kissed every five minutes. Sarah wondered doubtfully if they ever kissed each other. There was no escape in an air-raid shelter from the smells of tobacco, fart and sick and the coughing and snoring. Sarah would sometimes have preferred to have been outside of gasmasks and shelters and risk a German bomb, though there was always some cheerful chatter and banter, Jerry, Fritz and Kraut figuring largely. And there was her mother's warmth and proximity. Father always stayed at home, 'on fire-watching duty.'

It seemed the angels had taken Hayden when Mrs Morrison appeared one night at the shelter alone. The shelter community unanimously expressed their agreement that he was better off where he was and stayed silently thankful. Mrs. Morrison was comforted.

Sarah guiltily sighed with relief as she snuggled between her mother and her sister with eyes closed, loving the warmth of their bodies compared with the freezing cold bed she and her sister shared with the oven-plate, wrapped in a singed blanket, for their feet. Here the two sisters didn't have to fight for their share of the oven-plate. Queenie had a theory. She always had theories. 'Knowings' she called them. The one about the oven-plate was: 'if your feet are warm the rest of you will be.' Well, if 'the rest of you' went only as far as the ankles she was right.

Noticeably 'only guns' destroyed buildings and people. Much of the destruction was distant enough from Lime Street not to be intimate. But not always. The Davis's house on the end of the terrace was hit. The Davis family never came to the shelter preferring to cram the four children into a cupboard under the stairs. Much good it did them. Mr and Mrs Davis and their children Raymond, Arnold, Dorothy and Joan, gone in a flash. The dreaded doodlebug. One would hear a buzz overhead, then a few seconds of dry-mouthed silence, enough time to wonder. Like all the neighbourhood the Davis's would have been listening, stock still like statues, the children squashed together, waiting, scarcely breathing, then the crash. They could not say Thank God. Most people in the street had envied that house for its garden at the side being at the end of the row. Arnold Davis, Sarah's close friend, had dreamed and talked of being eleven and having his first pair of long trousers. The envied house was now half a house, faded flowered wallpaper facing the world as if caught unawares, intimate indoor things nakedly exposed to the outside. Their fate bewildered Sarah; it was a time for questions, mostly rebuffed. Why them, why not us? Where are they now? What was God doing at the time? Did they feel anything? How can you bury them if they're in bits? Sarah would miss them, especially Arnold who would never wear long trousers.

Bomb-sites, out of bounds, compensated richly for war-time dearth of toys. Compare a home-knitted stuffed ATS doll in khaki uniform and a rough hand-sawn, painted draughts set with half front rooms, bits of settees and stoves, amputated legs of tables and chairs, drunken sinks and tilting walls, a sudden new landscape beckoning the youngsters, their games of make-believe inexhaustible, the weeds awaiting their chance amongst the craters and rubble. Two miles from home the Fairey Aviation factory remained intact, bold as brass, intent on becoming McVities Biscuit factory.

There were few men around. The two daughters didn't know why their father never 'went to the war'. He fire-watched, whatever that was, at night with the older men. They were told it was because he had flat feet. They remained curious and a little ashamed. 'Aren't all feet flat?' they wondered.

Sarah often climbed up into the lime tree and watched, unseen, regular rhythmic to-ings and fro-ings. Sometimes a drama like when Mr Sidebotham opposite exposed himself to two giggling girls. Sometimes a harangue from Mrs Beatty who had five children, a husband at war, and a frequent male visitor. And the Rent Collector who had a false hand inside a black leather glove and popped in and out of each house, awash with tea and cash. Billy and his grandmother went hand in hand going who knows where, she talking to him as if he understood. Mrs Boot toiled with a donkey stone spreading beige on her wettened front step with a cloth to make the colour even, an obsessive daily ritual since few people had ever been seen to cross her threshold and most people on the street donkey-stoned their steps once a week, brushing them off in the meantime. Sarah perched, birdlike, her eyes and ears missing nothing, looking down on a world at once commonplace and fascinating, small yet everything. She felt as if she were waiting. Her compliance with her mother's desire for her to be unremarkable was suffocating but tolerable because she was waiting. Queenie's favoured phrases sat lumpen in her head. Before tests, exams, sports she would say, 'You can only do your best,' a long history redolent in the word 'only'; 'Just do what you can,' with resigned falling intonation, discouraging, a simple stultifying message parading as tolerance and understanding. Josie, for the time being, conditioned more readily than Sarah. Sarah had begun to be outstanding, except to her mother whose gift for ignoring the unwelcome compelled her daughter to silence.

Queenie knew that only time and space spared her family. She knew and she feared for her children. They were all soon to know that Jewish children elsewhere were being herded into gas chambers, and their mums and dads; grandparents were having gold fillings pulled out of their teeth and gold rings removed from fingers which had been broken and beaten so as not to indent the gold. Picked over. Impregnated with the accumulation of the history of her forbears Queenie did what she did and said what she said out of fear and love as had her parents; there may well be a next time and place. She knew she was difficult, moody, irritable. The ambience changed too frequently for stability. Queenie, for reasons the children scarcely knew, would suddenly go quiet, even tearful, and walk away from the tea table leaving the iced buns she often bought as a treat looking like fat greasy fingers.

The war raged on. And Leonard left them. Sarah and Josie spent many irresistible hours after bedtime sitting on the top stair listening to whispered rows. Such venom in a whisper. On no account were the children to hear. Here was an ordinary peaceable family. Sudden auditory cues alerted the daughters to take up their positions at the top of the stairs armed with a blanket. The normal hum of voices, or the radio, stops. Now new intonation with exaggerated emphasis on certain words: *she . . . her . . . . the children . . . . God's sake . . . . sick of . . . . money . . . . the kid . . . . not standing for . . . . your mother . . . . bloody Yids . . . .* and sizzling, indecipherable words either side of these spit out gobbets. The 'whisperings' fascinated and frightened the children even though they were always the same. Signals for the retreat to bed were another predictable part of the performance: silence, quick heavy footsteps, front door slammed, occasionally stifled sobbing. The frequency of the performance made it become part of normal life to the children. It was like listening to a story over and over again, knowing all the events, the dialogue and the ending, and still spellbound, waiting for the next time. Two children in bed, huddled together for warmth, always drowsily aware of the finale: the late slow heavy steps up the stair treads, a door closing quietly. The book closed again. Until one day the story changed. It had a different finale.

Sarah and Josie were expected to share their mother's shame and lies. They were to say he was working away. 'That would do for now', one of Queenie's favourite expressions reflecting her obsessive attention to the surface; a life, lived on the outside, a honed performance, the production the reality. Except the girls saw another show after the curtain came down. They were to know in certain terms that he was a wicked father who'd left their mother in the lurch to bring up two young children alone in terrible times. 'How could he? Such a burden.' Sarah had to become much older before wondering about the other side of the story. Queenie's outbursts were rare, cruel and memorable. Outside of them they were to play their parts on her stage. Even the grandparents were players. So Leonard had been temporarily transferred to a newspaper down London way. Everyone knew otherwise. No-one asked searching questions. And Queenie got a job in a dress shop, Seymour Modes, on Stockport Road. Mrs Fletcher with red hair and a flaming temper minded the girls after school. Wednesdays, half-day closing at Seymour Modes, meant walking straight home. No deviation of three hours with the fiery Mrs Fletcher but this time to a warm house, the fire lit, the smell of cooking and Queenie out of her smart black suit and white blouse shop assistant uniform. Sarah would love Wednesdays for ever.

Leonard never came back. People stopped asking after him. Grandmother Sophie spirited him out of existence. The time came when he was never mentioned. Except for once. "It would never have happened if you'd married a Jewish boy!" Grandmother's unguarded words blurted out and Sarah and Josie knew. Not what it meant but that they were Jews. It's not important, they were told. Better to keep quiet about it. Some people don't like Jews.

They hardly knew what it all meant and their questions were left in the air, or replied to with banal empty words: it's just another religion; no need to bother your heads about it; and you keep going to school prayers and hymns like all the others. Sarah had always envied the little group of children who were allowed to stay in the classroom and read on account of their different religions while the rest filed into assembly. She thought she might tell but something held her back. She was unaccountably nervous of being a Jew.

Chapter 2

A GENTLE TAP TAP ON the door to the apartment on Avenue Louis Blanc in northern Paris drifted into the slumbers of Claude's father, David. He sat upright in his armchair attentively wondering if the sound had been fanciful. His wife and children had gone to bed long since. It came again, a brittle, urgent tap tap tap. David leapt to his feet, glancing at the unlikely hour for visitors as he moved swiftly, in stocking-feet, through the hall.

'Who is it?' he whispered through the bolted door.

'David, let me in. It's Benjamin.'

David unlocked the door hastily to admit his oldest and dearest friend.

'Benjamin, come in, come in. What is it?'

The two men embraced. The vehemence of Benjamin's greeting frightened David. He felt the tautness of his friend's body.

'Come into the sitting room. Let me give you a cognac.'

'No David, it's not the moment. We are leaving. Now. You must do the same. Listen to me.' He spoke urgently. 'Take your family away while you still can. Now the Occupation of our country has begun it's going to be almost impossible to get out of here. The Hirsch family were taken by the Germans late last night. God knows where. All of them. The two children, their grandmother, the whole family forced out of the house, bundled into a van and driven away. David, you *must* take your family away from this madness. Think of them, your beautiful Lily, and darling children, Claude and Rose. Leave quickly, now!' Benjamin fiercely embraced his friend again, his face wet with tears. 'Leave now, before it's too late. Forget for now the ideals we share.' Benjamin paused to regain control of his voice. 'They count for nothing in the face of the lunacy around us. Be practical, now, David. It's time to be practical! Go!'

'Benjamin, my dear friend, the dreams we have shared for so long? Everything we have shared through literature, poetry, music? Our steadfastness through this terrible time?' David felt the tears spurting, his strength and resolve flowing away like an ebbing tide. 'Please stay a few moments.'

Benjamin complied and the two sat together in the old, comfortable chairs as they always had, the cognac on a small table at arm's length between them. In the few moments of silence as he poured two small glasses David scanned the pictures in his head of their friendship; the two families sharing their lives. Sometimes David's brother, Joseph and his wife, Mireille, would join them. David saw their walks to the synagogue, two close families. He saw Thursday evenings, he and Benjamin sharing Cognac and ideals in the Blum sitting room, the children, Claude and Rose, tucked up in bed; Lili, who always left them to it, knowing that there were matters, vital to them, which they would discuss; they would argue, agree, discover, as kindred spirits. There was no resentment on Lili's part. She had her own way of knowing things. David knew how she loved to hear the rise and fall of their discussions from her bed, too far away to catch the words. She often found words tiresome and unreliable, preferring to trust her feelings and intuitions. Thursday nights Benjamin would bring his cello and play for half an hour when Lili and the children, Claude and Rose, came down to listen, often to the Bach unaccompanied suites, occasionally some folk tunes. The family back in bed and the two men would talk of Verlaine, Hugo, Baudelaire, Proust, politics, the diaspora, the terrible times, the defeat and occupation of their country.

'I am leaving everything, David, everything I own, all my books, artefacts, paintings, everything. And my cello. I can no longer believe in the poetry I read, the ideals of the artist, the music I play, not in the world we live in. No! It's all hot air, belongs elsewhere, it's rubbish here and now!' Benjamin's large body was sweating and trembling now. He refused his usual top-up of cognac. His dark eyes blazed. 'Human beings are the most self-interested, cruel and brutish of all species. Do you know how many Jews have disappeared in this madness? Have you heard from the network what is happening to Jewish people? No. You wouldn't have. I've heard of Jews from all over being put on trains bound for Germany, plucked from their homes to work for Germany. I wonder what *that* means. There are terrible rumours flying around about just what that means. You have your head in the sand, my old friend. You sit there reading your poets and philosophers, discussing, playing music, running your business as if nothing is happening. What can all this do in the face of the brutality and brokenness of what we see and hear every day? Your painters and musicians are blind to the real world, idealistic. Their world is Utopia. Do you know what Utopia means, David? It means 'nowhere'. Benjamin talks rapidly. 'You must leave now. Your notions are for another day, maybe another world. They don't fit here and now. Maybe there is that better world, the one we dream of, or perhaps it's an illusion. Accept that David. *Now* it's time to save yourselves. You must *act.* You stay here and cling to your ideals and you'll be dead. All of you. You, Lili and the children. David, get out!'

'We have done nothing wrong, Benjamin. What have we done wrong?' David was dazed. 'We aren't interested in politics. In any case I've made contingency plans.' His utterance was lame and tearful.

'You can't say you are not interested in politics!' Benjamin shouted. 'You have to be interested, your life depends on it. Listen, David. The only plan worth anything is to go immediately.'

'And what of my shop, my business? All the jewellery and everything? Our life here!'

'You still have your lives, for God's sake, David. That's all that matters. And in any case it's only a matter of time before you'll be kicked out of your shop. Soon there'll be no-one walking into your shop to buy jewellery! It won't BE your shop! No Jew is safe here now. You can see what is happening around us. Your turn will come soon. People disappear. They say there's a list of people to be disposed of. We'll be on it, you can be sure. Can't you feel the fear all around us, the danger? It's terrible to have your country occupied.' Benjamin gulped and stemmed the tears knowing the urgency of his mission. 'It's not responsible of you to stay here, David. And if you don't go now you may never get out.' He felt anger, frustration and deep love. He stood up and stretched out his arms. David rose slowly and weightily from his chair. The two men hugged each other ardently, tearfully.

'Where will you go, Benjamin?'

'We're going into Spain first and then we'll try to get to England from there.'

'So far away.'

'Adieu, my dear friend. Please, please David, go quickly. Oh, dear God. May the God of Moses be at your right hand. Leave, LEAVE!'

They parted, fearful and despairing fellow Jews, their hearts heavy with their shared history.

David felt his heart thumping, his breath struggling, panic surging up through his body to somewhere behind his eyes. Anger quickly replaced his panic. He strode about the room spitting out words.

'God in heaven! What is this life? Renounce my ideals, my beliefs? For what, for whom? Run away Benjamin said. Again! Again! Always running away. This is my home. Our home . . . my family, my life. Why? Why? Will someone tell me what it all means, for God's sake? We came here to make a new home far from the Russian barbarians. Western Europe is a *civilised* place. Germany is a country of Bach, Beethoven, Schiller, Goethe.' David was shouting and sobbing. 'We, all the family, know nothing else but France. We are French. For heaven's sake my father died fighting for France in the Great War. Dear maman never left France in all of her life. How French do we have to be? God help us.' His voice tailed away to a whisper. 'And God in heaven, will my wife's family, her mother and her brother, Thierry, be prised out of their little house in Marseille? And put on a train? Because they're Jews? We're NOT leaving.' David sat in his chair, shaking. His raging conflict suddenly collapsed under a weight of sobbing. Disturbed by unusual sounds Lili came down to find her husband rocking himself in his chair to the rhythm of his sobbing. She knelt in front of him wrapping her thin arms around his bulky body to rock and cry with him.

'There there, David. We'll find a way.'

She moved her hand into his thick curly hair as they clung to each other, Lili the stronger in the deeply intimate embrace. She knew everything. She had known this time would come. Two days after was the Sabbath. They would celebrate as usual. Not as usual. She would try with all her strength to persuade David to take them all away from this.

Deep down in David's unconscious mind were premonitions, forebodings which would peak up into his awareness from time to time like pin pricks, painful and swift, yet powerful enough to generate contingency plans. Some time ago he had insisted that, together, he and his ten year old son, Claude, would take a regular walk along several streets as far as a little Catholic Pensionnat, an unremarkable drab grey building with tall slim shutters braided with crumbling green paint; a strange little walk to nothing in particular. Claude had wished for a park, a Punch and Judy show, le Théatre de Guignol, a river, an ice cream. But the walk was insistently the same. On several occasions David had entered the Pensionnat leaving Claude to wait outside, impatient to return home. Claude was satisfied with his father's explanation that he needed to talk to grown-up friends about serious matters.

David Blum knew things viscerally. He had a wordless sense of menace, but rationally held to beliefs in justice, liberty and equality. Everything surely had changed since his grandfather had arrived, penniless, from Russian pogroms, to find safety in France. The family had arrived in Paris to a welcome and offers of money from Jewish families who belonged to an international organisation committed to befriending any displaced Jews who were looking for help. They prospered and thanked their lucky stars. A successful business was built up by the grandfather and David's father thanks to contacts they found. David who was born into this flourishing bourgeois milieu could scarcely believe the provenance of his family and felt as thoroughly French as Maurice Chevalier. He 'married Jewish', a girl whose family had been in France for ever. She came from Marseille, from a family of generations of market traders. They met at a fine arts exhibition in the Place Vendome. David spotted her, a beautiful, dark-haired spanish looking young woman, rather frail and shy he thought. He asked her to join him for coffee in a nearby cafe. Her southern accent attracted him; she told him she had only been in Paris for a few weeks, her first visit, the start of her studies in the history of art. His family would disapprove and, indeed, when he told them some months later of their intentions to marry, his father, always direct, had told him he was sorry to see him marry beneath him. Nor was he too pleased when David laughed in his face. Mireille was soon to be accepted into this snobbish milieu, especially after having two beautiful children. But she always felt that they disapproved of her 'famille artisanale'. David took over the jeweller's shop when his father retired, had two children and felt as safe as houses. His parents had retired to a house in Honfleur, on the Normandy coast. They were glad to be out of Paris.

David pondered that he could have tried to move out of Paris to a safer place before the Germans invaded, when rumours of impending danger were growing. He had friends who had found refuge in England. There were people he had heard of, some he knew, who had disappeared overnight. But this was his home and he loved it. They had done no wrong. They would stay and see it through. No running away this time.

Soon Claude knew the walk to the pensionnat like the back of his hand, 'comme sa poche'. That was the intention. His father was satisfied and disturbed. At times his body felt the chinks in his beliefs. He explained to his son that one day he may be part of a big adventure and he would need to play his part like a grown-up. It would seem strange but he would see it would be for the best in the end. Claude was mystified but proud and liked the idea of an adventure. Rose would shortly be going to stay with her schoolfriend in Blois. The family weren't Jews so she'd be safe. Travelling these days was unpredictable so Lily would go with her to make sure she got there safely. David's doubts jabbed at him again when he knew that the family in Blois weren't Jews. 'It'll all be fine,' he repeatedly told himself and others. 'All this madness will soon be over and we can get back to normal.' Even he was beginning to glimpse the depths of his self-deception.

Chapter 3

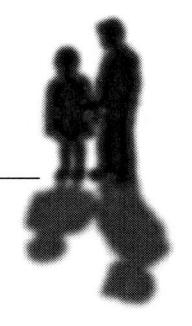

SARAH WAS CELEBRATING HER TENTH birthday in the air-raid shelter at the end of the street, listening to the thrumming sounds of destruction. The strident undulating air-raid warning siren had annoyingly interrupted her little party at home, summoning the neighbourhood to the dubious safety of the air-raid shelter, a routine occurrence lately. And many of the air-raid warnings were false alarms. Few complained. Everyone said it was better to be safe than sorry. The high-pitched monotone of the 'all-clear' siren was always so long in coming, a harsh sustained wail sounding like music to anxious ears.

At this point in her life Sarah did not know she was a Jew. No-one had said and today she was ten. It soon became clear that there would be no party tonight. Sarah was less concerned about an air-raid than about having no candles to blow out on her birthday cake cleverly made by her mother from their frugal rations. It was 7.30pm and they had been packed into the air-raid shelter since about 4pm, long enough for the comforting cake and drinks to have been consumed, for the air to be thick with the smell of tobacco smoke and urine and for the banter to have died down. It was strictly forbidden to leave the shelter before the 'all-clear' but a few, now impatient and reassured by the increasingly distant sounds of the blitz, (measuring sound against distance without instruments, had become a precise auditory skill), groped their way furtively in pitch black to the familiar comfort of their homes, either to stay there or to find something useful to do to take back to the shelter. Queenie chose this night to return home briefly to bring back the little birthday cake and more of her sewing. She was always sewing, irresistibly needing to fabricate with her hands, releasing her from fabricating with her mind, doing something useful to block out the horror and fearfulness of the war and the turmoil in her head.

The two girls waited anxiously for her return. It had been a long stint in the shelter. Sarah and Josie were missing the treat of the comfort and warmth of their mother's small slim body, her homely fragrance and rare softly reassuring words. The siren, for many, was the blaring signal of indiscriminate destruction, a devil sound which filled bodies and minds with dread. For Queenie's two daughters it signalled a mother's closeness, a tender time, a warmth they scarcely knew. They loved the air-raids for their gift of intimacy, dissipated all too quickly by the 'all-clear', their mother's sharpness again, the sound of the raucous monotone communicating safety, for the time being, over vast distances. Queenie's keen edges seemed to smooth off every time they settled into their habitual place in the shelter. Then the sound of the 'all-clear' was like a honing guide, finding the soft places to chisel back into their customary serpent-tooth sharpness.

Queenie was a long time bringing back her sewing and the cake. Sleepiness, snoring, whispered exchanges, and dulled senses were suddenly, brutally jolted by explosions all round them. Screams and smoke filled the shelter which trembled throughout its joints and lost its light. The rubric said 'stay in your shelter if you hear an explosion.' They all did, cowering like trapped animals; dry mouthed, appealing to God as a last resort. Except for Mr Mottram who was bent on being a hero. He would go out and return to tell everybody what was happening. Lime Street, Harborne Street, Henderson Avenue, a bit of Stockport Road and Zion Congregational Church were in flames, an inferno, everything so familiar transforming into an alien landscape. Two fire-watchers came into the shelter to shout 'stay put!' until the fires had died down. Mr Mottram was found dead, broken and burnt black, in front of what was once 11 Lime Street, his bachelor home. Sarah and Josie, given to obeying, stayed in the smoky, cough and prayer filled shelter, breathing shallowly in the dark, terrified by the sound of explosions and falling buildings, still waiting for their mother to return. Some more people left, no longer able to restrain the need to see and find and know. Others were crying, wondering, thankful to be alive, holding hands, their bodies pulled inwards from fear and shock. Someone was incessantly repeating, 'Oh, God. Oh, God. Oh, God.' Words of comfort were half-heartedly offered to the children. A candle was lighted. The 'all-clear' hadn't gone. Queenie might still be soft and loving if only she would come back to the shelter. Josie would stay and wait for her. Sarah could wait no longer. She crept unseen out of the gloom of the shelter, into the flame-lit night; fires, smoke, rubble, buildings still tumbling, giving up the ghost. How would she find her mother, and would she be warm and tender or sharp and brittle? So much frantic activity and noise; men and women with shovels and picks, hands grovelling, shouting to find life amongst wreckage, or even trace bits and pieces to be identified. Names were called out, then waiting for responses, ears pressed against the debris, grownups crying, unaffected now by the sound of toppling buildings around them. Fire engines screamed onto the scene. So much smoke, and sudden flames devouring a precious belonging, a drawer of clothes, a length of curtain, a rag rug, a bit of a person once touched and kissed, to be shovelled away with the rubble; firemen dousing blazing remnants of homes; St. John's Ambulance Brigade tending the wounded and covering the dead; a scene of wanton destruction and wretchedness filling Sarah's bewildered senses.

'Mum! Where are you? Where are you? Mum . . . . !' Sarah ran amongst the fire and smoke and rubble, screaming for her mother and not knowing where 18 Lime Street was anymore. There were some houses still standing but now unrecognisable lacking their familiar context. The 'all-clear' sounded, wailing above the din of human panic, grief, frantic scraping and clawing, shouts of names, instructions, howling. For once the 'all-clear' was scarcely heeded.

'Mum! It's Sarah! I love you, I don't mind if you're cross. Mum!' She was running down what she thought would be her street. A neighbour, a St John's Ambulance man and a friend of the family, scooped her up into his arms and took her to his elderly mother's home nearby; Regal Street, a street still standing, now at last living up to its name, amongst the devastation. He had found Sarah soon enough for her not to see the remains of her mother, and others. Mr Williams was busy, had no time for niceties and no sooner deposited Sarah than was back into the hell of his neighbourhood, set on finding Josie.

Fairey Aviation factory remained defiantly intact. Queenie was found dead at what would have been the front door of her home, clutching a cake tin and a carpet bag containing her treasured sewing materials.

Mrs Williams put Sarah and Josie to bed that night in her own double bed which still held the warmth of her body and her stone hot water bottle. She was one of many who steadfastly refused to leave their homes during a blitz. She wouldn't have been sleeping, she'd have been waiting for the 'all-clear' and for her son to return. Now she would sit in her armchair mindful of two youngsters who were safe upstairs, who had drunk cups of hot milk flavoured with ersatz chocolate and who had fallen into exhausted sleep. She had assured them that their mother would be found and that tomorrow was another day. She would watch the flames and smoke through her front room window and listen to the unfamiliar sounds of raw emotions.

Her son returned with the news that Queenie had been just recognisable. He had brought back her sewing bag which he had had to prise from the grip of her dislocated hand.

The two girls stayed with Mrs. Williams and her ambulance-man son for a day and a night, long enough for arrangements to be made to take them to their grandparents on the other side of the city.

Chapter 4

HABITUAL PREPARATIONS FOR FRIDAY NIGHT Sabbath eve supper continued but, for once, joylessly for David and Lily. David toiled inside his head. 'How could anyone be sure? And anyway, if Benjamin were right, where could we go, not to be found again? All our money is invested in the shop. Others have sold up and gone long since. Businesses have been closed down and plundered, I know that. But maybe these people had done something wrong. Perhaps they had been too precipitate, too rash, too calculating, forever running, fleeing, always fearful. That's no way to live. I have stood my ground, firm in my beliefs, determined that France is the home for my family, the country my grandparents had adopted for the safety of their family. What would they think if I uprooted now, I wonder?'

Misgivings stabbed into his guts as he prepared the candles for his wife to light, a mitsvas reserved for her. He called Claude and Rose from their game of Happy Families to come to the table. His wife began to adorn the table with home-baked braided loaves of bread, the challa, crispy outside and soft inside, only cut after the blessing, a tureen of noodle soup, chopped liver, celery, radishes, olives and chicken with apple sauce. The bread was nearly black due to the poor flour. The chicken was scrawny and tough, scarcely enough on it for all of them. The rest came from their friends' gardens or from hoarded tins and jars. Whatever was available Lily seemed able to make Friday night supper into a special meal, a celebration worth waiting for after the plain repetitive fare of the rest of the week. Even the ersatz coffee went down well. One precious bottle of wine was taken from a store which David, with foresight, had built up. His many premonitions arose out of a stratum of fear laid down by successive generations. Be prepared for the next reckoning. He was not a doom-laden man but always poised in readiness. He was often teased by Lily for his 'siege mentality', all the time hoarding tins of vegetables, anchovies, tomatoes, olives. He loved to preserve fruit and mushrooms in jars. They looked increasingly uninviting, sitting on shelf above shelf in the pantry. But Lily was often heard to say, never go on appearances. She was right, mostly.

It was the time for David to say prayers to bless his wife and the children and to welcome the Sabbath angels who sing 'May your coming be in peace, and may you depart in peace.' He wondered, now in his head, if he had risked the lives of his family through his caution, his faith that good would triumph, his proud condemnation of the rashness of his safely departed friends.

His mind was in turmoil. He seemed to have no control over it. Again his thoughts tumbled around his head: 'Why should we always be uprooting? Some sinister hand always pushing us to far-flung places with different languages, different cultures to absorb and be absorbed. How can we ever become a 'normal' people if, for two millennia, we've been wandering in exile, tolerated? We need to stand our ground. People have their own ideas about what will be good for them. How can we know if these are better or worse than the convictions told to you, in good faith, by those who care for you? And yet, and yet I altered the clock.'

His jeweller's shop was the part of the ground floor which fronted onto the street. He had carried out the transformation of the clock mindlessly, just in case; another premonition. He had lovingly removed the clock's innards and stored the pendulum, weights and mechanism in the large cupboard housing repair work, mostly clocks and watches. At least the smallest member of his family could be hidden, should the unlikely need arise and he would know exactly what to do. Two years ago his daughter, Rose, would have fitted into a clock. She had grown so quickly. Even though only eleven one could see the beautiful woman she would become, dark and slim like her mother. The safest thing for her would be to take her to friends who were not Jewish. Both children would be safe. They would all be fine.

As he sat at the table with his family suddenly he felt his breath shortening, his guts tightening, his vision blurring. He knew, in a sickening moment, that he had appallingly lacked foresight, that he had been wrong. He had made the terrible decision to stay in Avenue Louis Blanc, assuring his wife of their safety. Lili had had serious doubts about the wisdom of remaining in Paris. She feared the Germans, tramping their streets, taking over everything, often boastful and bullying in the way they treated their victims, and was aware of some amongst their acquaintances who were rather too helpful to the occupiers of their country, a fact which heaped more shame than already felt. Then there was the fear from the trickling information coming from Germany about even more restrictions and removal of Jews. And recently the sudden disappearance of some Jewish families. Lily understood the flight of some of their friends and others they had heard tell of. She feared terribly for her children and said as much to David. He had seemed so sure and so proud she had finally acquiesced, believing her husband to be more worldly wise than she and feeling ashamed she lacked his courage. It was not her habit always to give in to her husband's wishes, far from it. But this was not a matter for discussion and compromise. She knew, quite simply, David would never leave. She would talk to him tomorrow about getting the children down to Marseille to their grandmother where they'd be safer. She would perhaps go with them though reluctant to leave David. She was anxious, too, to see her mother again after the long separation because of the travel restrictions. Her brother Thierry who lived with their mother had managed to communicate that Alice was increasingly frail and downhearted. She had always refused to leave her little house in the suburbs of Marseille and did not even contemplate moving to live with her family in Paris when they had invited her years ago when their father died. At least Thierry was there, on and off, to keep an eye on her.

David, full of foreboding, sipped the wine which would sanctify the Sabbath and began his prayers.

The ceremonial absorption was halted by the screech of car brakes outside their building, brutally cutting short David's voice.

Three doors banged shut. Next, the rhythmic pounding of resolute footsteps, plainly not those of usual visitors. David pulled Claude unceremoniously from his chair. 'Your big adventure has just begun!' he whispered loudly as he hastily rushed him through the adjoining door into the shop and installed his child in the clock. 'Keep your promises! I love you. Au revoir.' Within seconds he had returned to the dining room where Lili, knowingly, had already removed every trace of Claude's supper.

From inside his dark carapace Claude heard the peremptory rapping on their entrance door, his father's strangled 'j'arrive, j'arrive,' their quiet acknowledgement that they were Monsieur et Madame Blum and, yes, this was their daughter, Rose. He heard his mother firmly asserting that their son was staying with friends in Tours, his father asking what they had done wrong; he heard cupboard doors banged, drawers slammed, tramping feet, his father repeating: 'What have we done wrong?' He was told to be quiet or it would be the worse for him and his family. Someone opened the adjoining door into the shop. Silence. Then a few heavy footsteps and the door to the only cupboard in the shop roughly opened displaying the innards of Claude's clock. Silence. Then footsteps back into the apartment and the door slammed behind them. 'Who are these people, strutting around all our rooms, and making so much noise?' Claude's mouth was dry, his body rigid, his unblinking eyes staring fearfully at blackness. He whispered, 'Papa, I don't like this adventure. Come and get me, I'm frightened. Tell them to go. Papa? Papa?' He desperately wanted to shout out, even push open the door of the clock and run into the dining room straight to his mother but he was paralysed by his fear and the promise he had made.

'What right do you have?' Claude had never heard his father's voice say words in that way, aggressive yet pleading.

'Shut up. You are leaving.' Sounds of scuffling.

'There is no need to push us,' David shouted. 'Come my darlings. Come on. Do as they say. At least we are together.'

The door banged shut. A few moments later Claude heard an engine start up, a car move off, its sound disappear. 'And me? I'm not together with you. I want to go with you. Wherever that may be. Please!' Claude sobbed. 'Let me go with you, papa, I don't like it. Why did you make me promise? You've left me all on my own!' Claude was now shouting and banging his fist on the clock door. 'You've just left me all on my own in the dark!' He could no longer shriek for the sobbing. He covered his face with his hands, his body shaking all over.

In spite of his anguish he held steadfastly to his promise that he would stay there, whatever he heard. And when he heard no-one he would remain in the clock case as instructed, for as long as it would take him to peel and eat the two oranges which he would find near his feet. Only then would he come out and go quickly, without speaking to anybody, to the Pensionnat on the well-trodden route. There Father Michel would be waiting for him.

The tears dried up but the tightness in his throat and shoulders got worse. He felt cold and afraid as he stood stock still in the confined blackness. 'Where have they gone? What's happening? When are you coming back for me?' He didn't feel like eating oranges. And in any case he couldn't reach down to get them. 'Papa, you forgot; I can't bend down in here.' He would take his oranges with him to the Pensionnat, two bright orbs to comfort him till he saw his family again. The silent darkness engulfed him, relieved by the faint competing rhythms of the ticking clocks in the shop, the chirpy cuckoo now and then and the delicate silvery chimes of the carriage clocks. He knew that the big chimes were always silenced until given voice when a customer showed interest.

His feet were now numb. The musty scent of the wood and polish began to feel suffocating. His tummy hurt. There was no light, nothing to look at, no space to move. 'Where are you? Where did you go to? Maman . . .' The ticking clocks now frantically competed with the strident voices of the intruders inside his head, 'Shut up! Move!' The strangled questions from his father, 'What have we done wrong?' The desperate 'please, please' of his mother and the guttural orders of strangers. The dark began to close down upon him taking his breath away, squeezing his thin body. Panic gripped his throat and the idea flooded his head: 'I could die in here. I'm going to die. Before I've kept my promise! Will I have a ghost? Ghost please go to the Pensionnat to keep my promise. Please, please.' He traced his trembling fingers on the surface of the wood of the clock door in front of him to remind himself of his way of escape and suddenly remembered how smooth and polished it was on the outside compared with the rough surface under his fingertips. His eyes searched wildly for something to see until they seized on a line in the blackness which was the top of the slightly ill-fitting clock door. The thin grey trace brought the shop into his head and calmed him: the counter with beautiful watches and bracelets gleaming gold and silver under their glass cover, the slim drawers under the counter, velvet lined, with flashing rings in slots waiting to be pulled out and proudly displayed, the carriage clocks standing on small feet on two of the shelves, the shop door with its gleaming door bell and hammer, the grandfather and grandmother clocks awaiting their moment to sing, standing straight backed against the far wall, his own eviscerated clock flanked on one side by two grandmothers and on the other by the connecting door into the apartment.

'Where are you now?' His voice was small. 'Don't leave me, maman. Please come back, please. Why did you leave me on my own?' Claude sobbed quietly into his palms. 'I love you, come back. I'll find you.' He thought of his promise to his father, so paramount, took a deep breath and resolutely concentrated on the clock.

He knew the long case clock in which he stood. It had come from England, made by Gillows of Lancaster, and was plainly carved and highly polished, with a long slender pendulum and shiny weights which had an eight day run. In spite of his fear Claude felt strangely excited. He imagined being the pendulum which had lodged there for well over a hundred years, only temporarily removed to give him a hiding place. Papa would soon reinstate the pendulum and mechanism when he returned. And everything would come back to normal. And he would never have to hide in the clock again, or go on that walk, or miss dinner, or be alone.

'Where are you? Papa, what is this adventure for? I don't like it, I don't want an adventure. I'm coming to find you.' He knew he had to move and go on to keep the next part of his promise.

Would he have peeled and eaten two oranges by now? Thin skinned oranges took more time than the thick skinned variety. He would stay longer in case his oranges were thin skinned and full of pips. And he had heard the cuckoo only twice.

Papa always said that supper was never a surprise to him. When he was ready to close up the shop he could often just detect the odour of cauliflower latkes, cheese strudel or whatever his wife had chosen for them. Claude could just detect the odour of the supper he had missed; noodle soup. spices, roast chicken, still on the table. He was not hungry but his body warmed with the smells of lovingly prepared food. He caught the scent of the newly made bread, a scent he associated so strongly with his mother when she caressed him. He saw his father's crystal wine glass gleaming its dark rich contents, and remembered there had not been time to finish the prayers. He wondered if the candles would still be alight. Maman would be upset by the waste of good food. She always saved left-overs, carrot tops, vegetable stock, a lettuce leaf for her wonderful soups.

Perhaps they would all return later just in time to eat their supper before the Sabbath began at sunset. He would stay longer in the clock, just in case. He felt calmer, even a bit numb. He could breathe more freely and remembered that, months ago, his father, with remarkable prescience and foreboding, after emptying the clock casing of its pendulum and mechanical parts, had drilled holes in the back of the case.

A promise was made and promises were inviolate as he had often heard said in his family. In any case he was now cold and pins and needles jabbed into his legs. He could have eaten six tight skinned oranges by now. It was time to keep his promise and walk, not run, to the Pensionnat. The family hadn't returned. He opened the clock door, stepped out into the dark grey light, stamped his feet and turned back to pick up his oranges and put them in his trouser pockets.

He gazed round the shop. It was smaller and more intense than he had seen in his mind's eye. The dazzling gleams of gold, silver, brass and copper leapt out of the darkness. He had never seen the shop look so magical. He was transfixed, lost in a few absorbing moments. As his eyes adjusted to a colder light he saw the connecting door and tiptoed towards it. Perhaps they would all be there at the table, waiting for him. And they would shout Hurrah, Well Done, and they would all embrace and laugh.

The candles were still alight, nearly spent, the food untouched, the silence palpable. He lingered for a moment thinking how upset his mother would be at such a waste of good food, how his father may be thinking he need not have opened the bottle of wine, that Rose had missed her favourite apple sauce. 'They may be back tonight for their supper.' He closed the door behind him and set off on his versed route to the school.

Claude thrust his hands into his trouser pockets, for all the world casual as he left the apartment. 'Don't run!' His hands clasped the two oranges, his only link now with his family. He pressed them harder and harder until their juice began to escape. He arrived at his destination cold and frightened and in a strange way detached from what was happening to him. Father Michel opened the front door of the school and gently hurried Claude into the dimly lit hall.

'Vite, vite, mon enfant.' He guided the boy into a vast, candle-lit refectory with two rows of trestle tables and benches. 'Sit down with me, Claude.' His gentle voice whispered around the lofty space as they sat opposite at the end of the table. 'I am Father Michel. We are all here to help you.' Claude took his two squashed oranges from his pockets and pressed them hard against his closed eyes and tear-stained cheeks. The juice ran over and between his lips and suffused his nostrils as he possessively pressed the fruit into his face.

'I want to go home now, please. I know the way. You don't need to come with me. They may be back now,' he whispered in a tiny controlled voice, pressing the oranges harder into his eyes. Father

Michel could scarcely hear the words. He delicately removed the oranges from the tight fists and looked at a thin child with dark eyes almost too big in his small white face. His short black hair stood up in tufts. He was small for his age, vulnerable, a waif who had been forced to stray. The Father knew the family had been taken. They had committed the crime of being Jews. As he looked at the child, the innocent, uncomprehending prey of evil, he momentarily questioned his faith. Claude eyed the tall elderly man, ascetic, straight backed, clothed in a black robe. His silvery hair was cropped, accentuating the bony angles of his face. If it were not for the bright blue smiling eyes he might look intimidating. Claude fixed his eyes on the ring which stood out hugely from the tangle of thin crossed fingers resting on the table. He had never seen a ring like that in his father's shop. He thought it drab with its upstanding dull gold signet etched into an insignia of intertwining letters; no diamonds, emeralds; no sparkle. At the same time Father Michel noted the good clothes on the boy, not those of a waif and stray; a thick grey cotton shirt buttoned up to the neck and a dark school coat of the best quality wool. Claude wondered why this man was called Father. Father he may be but not his father, short, plump, moustached with a head of crisp curly black hair.

A rotund Father Dominic appeared with a tray; hot vegetable soup, a chunk of homemade bread, and welcoming reassurance; the simple acts and words of untinged compassion which jolted Father Michel out of his misgivings. The elderly, large Father Dominic wiped Claude's face with the napkin from the tray and encouraged the boy to eat.

'We must stoke up your fire so that it will burn brightly.'

Claude noticed he was hungry. He ate his soup and bread voraciously, not looking at either of his companions. When he had finished he raised his head and looked from one to the other.

'Will you tell papa I don't like my adventure? Will they come and take me back home now?'

Father Dominic assured him they would help him all they could, and wondered how they would explain to this child his brutal dislocation. Urged to be patient and to say nothing of his family for the time being Claude was taken by candle light to a bed in a large room full of occupied beds. He silently undressed and was clothed in a long scratchy nightshirt. One of the Fathers lifted him into his bed and covered him up. Latin prayers were breathed over him like spells. There he was left, afraid of the whispering people in black robes, wondering why he needed help.

'Papa, maman, Rose, where are you? Come and find me now. I've done what you asked me to do.'

Within seconds Claude slept, exhausted. Father Dominic returned to perform his nightly task of casting an eye over all the sleeping children to be sure all was well. It was one of his favourite duties. On this occasion he entered the dormitory anxiously, wondering if the little Jewish boy had settled. He went straight away to look at the small, curled up shape occupying such a tiny space in the bed, and pondered about his future, and the future of his race. He fought back tears as he tiptoed along the aisle between two rows of iron beds, glancing at each pupil as he left, spending a few moments in prayer by the bed of their other protégé, Alfred Schumacher, and feared grievously for him, too.

Chapter 5

The Granddaughters

THE MOMENT MRS WILLIAMS HEARD the girls awake she called to them to come down. She fried bread and dried egg for them and told them as best she could that their mother was dead. Both of them were inconsolably silent. Josie ate her breakfast and played 'solitaire' all day. Sarah obligingly ate a corner of her fried bread, thanked Mrs Williams and set about sorting through the sewing bag, examining in detail every item. She stroked the smoothness of the wooden darning mushroom, opened and closed the flannel needle case, sniffed the leather case with a fancy handle marked Blackpool and containing a pair of scissors, fingered a piece of fuse wire which helped thread needles, an end piece of Sunlight soap to rub along a hem to make a permanent crease. There were a few bits of tailor's chalk, a wad of fents, a black pencil to make white cotton black, a velvet pin cushion, rubber buttons, saved elastic, press studs, hooks and eyes, and the half made white blouse which now would never be finished. It was as if Sarah were talking to her mother. In the future the sewing bag would become a source of comfort, a means to acknowledge her mother's love always there underneath the surface and embodied in a sewing bag.

Sophie and Daniel would learn later that morning, from their local police station, that their daughter, Queenie, had been killed, that the two grandchildren were safe, and that they were to expect the girls to arrive the following day. Indeed, that they were now responsible for Sarah and Josie.

Daniel and Sophie were desolate; now both their children dead, in unnatural ways. Daniel retreated into silence amidst the noisy anguish of Sophie all around him. Crying and ranting she crashed about in the kitchen preparing food with no particular dish in mind; frying onions, chopping carrots and leeks, boiling a chicken carcass for the stock, peeling potatoes, putting white haricot beans to soak. Such frantic activity released some anger and despair. Next she would clean their small terraced house from top to bottom. Daniel knew his Sophie. He would wait a while till she had slowed down, quietened before he intervened.

'Sophie. Maiden, my maiden. Come and sit quietly with me. We need to think about having Sarah and Josie with us.'

Sophie, tied to her culinary habits even, and especially, in extremis, turned down her stock, removed the onions from the gas and only then coming to sit with Daniel at their square, well-scrubbed kitchen table. Daniel reached across the table and took her hands. She was calmer. He still found her extraordinarily beautiful, her raven black hair now liberally stranded with white, her eyes as black and shiny as they were when she was a young girl, her vitality undiminished. She was glorious. He loved her with a passion and wondered what she saw in him. 'I will sing to her tonight,' he thought. 'She loves that. I'll sing You Are My Heart's Delight, her favourite.' It was a dark time to be sugared with sentimental songs.

'Sophie, love. Sarah and Josie, too, are distraught. They have only us and we must turn our thoughts to making a home here for them. They need us now and they'll be here tomorrow.' Spohie's head and shoulders slumped. 'Sophie, my love, why don't we, together, prepare our second bedroom for them, make it as welcoming and pretty as we can. Tonight I can make two bedspreads out of the material I bought for our front room curtains. You remember, it's heavy cotton folkweave, cream with embossed blue flowers. And we'll use the linen sheets and pillowcases we keep for just in case. We'll put some of our coat hangers in the wardrobe and line the chest of drawers with my pattern paper. You could polish the old brass lamp till it shines like a farthing. There won't be much room for us all but we can manage. We will do, for them, our grandchildren, what we didn't do for our own children. They will go to Bury Grammar School and be stars. They know they are Jews and they'll be proud of it. No more hiding.' Sophie looked up.

'God help them, Daniel. We did our best, the best we knew.'

Tears softened Sophie's eyes as he began to sing to her:

'You make my darkness light

When like a star you shine on me . . . .'

Sophie loved him with a passion and wondered what he saw in her. After the song Sophie said, tearfully, 'thank you, Daniel. Yes.'

There was a long silence as they looked at each other, holding hands across the table.

'Life is so hard, Daniel. When you think of our parents and what they went through to get here. And bring us up here. And then Ada who was just a lost soul. And now Queenie.'

Sophie straightened up and wiped her eyes on her sleeve.

'Well, let's get on with it then. We'll do our very best.'

The granddaughters arrived with only the clothes they stood up in, all carefully washed, dried and ironed by Mrs, Williams in an astonishingly short space of time, whilst they, clothed in blankets and socks, shared the blazing kitchen-grate fire with a clothes maiden draped in damp clothes, and obligingly ate soup and bread. Mrs. Williams did her best to insulate them from the sounds of an upside down world outside by switching on the Light Programme on the wireless but soon switched off, jarred by the inappropriate jingle-jangle of the latest favourites. As they left her in tears she could no longer keep back she gave each of them a new lace-edged handkerchief.

It was a long time before the two girls could talk about their mother. They settled in quickly and without complaint in the early days of their lives with their grandparents. They were used to a small house, a shared bedroom and no privacy. But this house was even smaller than their now non-existent house, especially as one of the two rooms downstairs was used as the workshop. They had one set of drawers for their clothes and two coat hangers each. That first night, after a meal of thick vegetable broth and bread, they went to bed and both sat upright, staring into darkness, and wept as silently as they could. Their grandparents had been so kind they didn't want to upset them. Sarah and Josie had never embraced, always keeping their distance, living inside themselves. Suddenly Josie whispered loudly, 'bugger it!' and disappeared under the bedclothes, her crying over. Sarah cried herself to sleep. They were unable to comfort each other.

Sophie knew they were too quiet. The tiny house was now overcrowded and both girls were well aware that their presence had changed the quiet routine lives of these two elderly people. There was no longer the cut and thrust they had been used to at home. Though Sophie often snapped at them it would be, in their view, unfair to snap back at her. Sophie and Daniel waited, whilst gently mentioning Queenie, mum, how she was now safe from hurt, would want her daughters to be happy, how she always enjoyed her lie-in on Sunday mornings, how she loved to check her Littlewooods pools every Saturday night, dreaming of riches, how she always loved to look smart; many small acknowledgements to keep the memory of her alive and prevent her being consigned to silence. The two granddaughters hugged their own memories and feelings to themselves, unshared.

The grandparents were loved and loving. The house was humble, fronting onto the street, a peg down from Lime Street, having no front garden and privet hedge. It was called a two-up two-down. One-down was the kitchen, the place where they ate, washed at the sink, sat in front of the black-leaded grate, bathed in a tin bath once a week, by arrangement, did homework after the table was cleared, talked. The window looked out onto a small backyard with a privy and a coal bunker and not even a hint of greenery. Two-down was Daniel's workshop, a methodical miracle. Bales of cloth filled half the space leaving the rest for a cutting table, machine area, and an ironing board which lived in a cupboard, to be let out and down when required, and a tailor's dummy; no space for chairs except a small stool in front of the sewing machine; chalks and cottons, pins and needles, scissors, machine accessories, all the tools of the trade nestled in a wall cupboard labelled in coloured order. There was scarcely room to move especially now that Daniel had taken on an apprentice, Joseph Blum, to give more time to Sophie for their girls, and to help this young man who had wisely fled from France with his wife and child at a time of profound unease. Daniel was a thread in a network of Jewish people ready to soften the landing of those in flight from Europe. Sophie boiled up. 'Where's the work coming from, I ask you? You've taken on a young man whose English sounds like Chinese and doesn't know the warp from the weft! You'll be falling over each other in that room. D'you think you're rich as Cresus? Oy, oy, oy!' Funds and 'ways and means' from the Jewish community were forthcoming, Joseph Blum learnt quickly and Sophie simmered.

The girls found the grandparents so much softer and allowing than ever their mother had been. Sophie sharpened her tongue sometimes but the girls learnt to know the fleetness of her edge. She had a new chance to bring up children differently from the way she had dealt with her own. Time had passed and times had changed. She would let them flourish, her Jewish girls.

At Daniel's insistence they all went together to watch the films of the opening of concentration camps. They read the reports, saw the newspaper pictures and could not speak. The unspeakable had taken place. Dead skeletal heaps of innocence piled high, and a few souls still clinging to life. More than enough unconscionable scrap. People left the cinema silently except for the sound of quiet sobbing. The family walked home together, had tea in the kitchen and the girls went to bed. There were no words. Not another word was spoken until the next morning. The images were etched into their minds for always.

Both girls passed their Eleven Plus and did well at the girls' grammar school. And they were exempted from morning assembly, a great source of pleasure. Quite a few Jewish girls, two Plymouth Brethren girls, and three Catholics enjoyed the chat and the chance to finish off homework. Josie would not be persuaded to stay on into the sixth form in spite of excellent General Certificate results.

Life was not easy for the girls at Pendleton Street and for different reasons. Josie's adolescence was charged with shame. No mother or father; the two people who turned up for parents' meetings at school were old and grey and looked as if they had come to the wrong meeting. Josie would let fly at Sarah in the privacy of their half-mile walk from where the school bus dropped them off.

'Oh, God, it's so embarrassing! I can't even take friends home. Even you, Miss Goody Two Shoes, don't bring your friends home. The front room's a sweat shop and the kitchen is so bloody old fashioned—a sodding great cast iron stove takes up a ton of space and belches smoke out like a bloody chain smoker!' Josie's rebelliousness was eloquent in its own way. 'And two old crows pecking about! My friend Shirley, her house has got a garden, a modern gas stove, a sitting room where you can sit. They've got Wedgwood ornaments in a display cabinet. Her mum and dad go dancing and they've got a bottle of sherry on their sideboard with little glasses, cut glass, next to it. And Shirley can go to the Palais de Dance on a Saturday night, dressed up and with make-up on. She's got at least three lipsticks, a powder compact, and a bottle of California Poppy. *And* She's got a dance frock and high heels. I couldn't go to the Palais even if I was allowed. What the hell would I wear? My school uniform? My best tweed suit they made for me? I'd rather go in my birthday suit!' Sarah had heard it all before and knew better than to try to defend her grandparents, their ways and their home.

'And I'm sick of wearing 'tailored garments',' said with a sneer. 'I want to buy something off the bloody peg and have some decent shoes with heels and fifteen denier stockings. I'm getting out of this sodding school uniform and white socks as soon as I can, you watch me. Oh, I know they've been kind and sacrificed a lot for us, blah,

blah, blah. God knows you've told me often enough. But it all makes me want to scream and break loose. Sick of it, I am. Sick, sick, sick!' Often there would be tears shed and wiped away before they reached the front door of 103 Pendleton Street.

When Daniel told her she was not going to London and she had to stay on at school she could no longer spare them and burst out:

'You've no bloody right to tell me what to do! I'm out of this, it's a can of worms. I'm going. Don't call us we'll call you, got it? There's a big world out there, you know, and it doesn't revolve round you! You've just got no spunk! Looking at me like I was something the sodding cat brought in . . . .' The cork had jumped out of the bottle.

No-one speaks. Daniel stares at the deal table as if he's examining the contours of the grain. Sarah bites her bottom lip to prevent her shouting back. Sophie pierces Josie with her jet eyes, twitches her shoulders and lips in preparation for her own onslaught when another tirade breaks loose.

'That's the last time I sit round this table with Granddad sloshing a glass of wine, and muttering praise this and praise that and singing some bloody chant about angels!'

'That's that, lady!' Sophie snaps. 'I don't know where you get your loud mouth from. Not our side of the family, that's for sure. Your dad, most likely. Well you can just start learning to keep your mouth shut in this house. You need it washing out with soap after all that terrible language, my girl. I've never heard the likes.'

'I don't need to learn anything from you. I'm out of here as fast as I can.' Josie's anger subsides into sobbing and desperate little gasps, 'I don't get it,' managed between breaths. 'Mum didn't want us two to be Jews. She thought it was better, safer. And now we *are* Jews. You should have left it as she wanted it. How am I supposed to know what to think? And when is it, or isn't it, OK to lie?'

'Your mum did what she thought best,' said Daniel as he put his arm around her shoulders, prepared, unnecessarily, to be pushed away. Sophie moved to put the kettle on the hob and to hide her tears. If only we had the chance, she thought, to go back in time and have a second go at it all.

'Listen Josie.' Daniel wanted to make it alright for his granddaughter, to smooth the ruffled feathers. 'You are a Jew. You're part of our race, whether you like it or not. You don't have to believe in the faith—but you are a Jew and you can't run away from that. Your mum did what she did thinking she was protecting you from—well, perhaps from the fate of those we saw in the film.' There followed a heavy silence.

'But what does that mean, Granddad, being a Jew?'

'You are chosen.'

'Chosen? Are you kidding? Chosen to be hounded and gassed? I don't buy that, I don't even begin to know what you're on about. Chosen? Don't make me laugh. So why have we had this bloody stupid war when six million of us 'chosen people' were rubbed out? Tell me that. Yes, 'chosen'—chosen to be murdered. And it's gone on for donkey's years. And it'll go on for more donkey's years. Count me out. It's beyond me and I'm off. I'm off to find folk who don't give a bugger about it all.' Josie fled upstairs to cry angry, bewildered uncomprehending tears into her pillow.

If she'd had a choice she'd rather have been black than Jewish; more exotic. Her mission was to be exotic, to flee the drabness of Cheetham Hill, the oldness of her grandparents, the stuffiness of her elite grammar school, the Jew thing, the mention of her mother. London would do for now. Paris and New York would come later. She would become Jasmin StClair.

Undaunted by huge opposition she set off for London as soon as she left school. The grandparents had no choice but to give her the fare and a little extra to be going on with and sent a letter to the

Youth Hostel at Battersea to secure bed and breakfast for a month. They had no choice in the face of the threats issued by Josie if they did not; throwing herself under a bus, going on the streets, hitching a lift to London. Josie knew how to get her way. Euston station, a buzz of people like bees in a hive; the underground and its map of many colours to negotiate; Battersea and a triumphant arrival at the youth hostel; welcoming faces and the talk of jobs. Josie took it all in her stride, her excitement and sense of freedom outweighing any fears of the unknown. Her over-riding anxiety was that she thought she looked unsophisticated, stodgy, gawky even. She smoked her first cigarette the evening she arrived and had her hair cut in a conspicuously short bob the next morning. With more enthusiasm she had ever felt in her life she set about becoming 'chic'. Taking a job at Lyon's Cornerhouse she promised herself great things to come. She would soon learn how to speak with a Cockney accent, how to jump on and off tubes without having to look at the map, how to wear with a swagger tighter and more revealing clothes, how to smoke with nonchalance. She was loving her new world.

Sarah, too, felt burdened but not knowing why, only that she would stay and somehow stick by her grandparents. She caught glimpses of her mother in each of them and felt she belonged here. Manchester University was not far away. Beside her sister, Sarah thought of herself as a bit staid, incapable of passionate outbursts. She loved her family yet still she felt as if she were waiting for something, as she had so often felt as a child, perched in the lime tree feeling 'different', not knowing why. Watching the goings-on in the street she had experienced a sense of not belonging to the world around her. She was more at home in the tree than in the house with her family, even with her friends. Still now, no words came to her to explain.

Sarah knew some of her sister's frustration but was well aware her own route was through school. The difficulties in her new life in Cheetham Hill ranged around her memories of the lime tree, the sewing bag, Billy knocking on the door to ask Queenie if her sister (Sarah) could come out to play; Queenie pleased by the mistaken relationship even though made by 'Ah poor Billy'; the disappearance of Lime Street, number eighteen, its tree, privet hedge, soldierly gladioli. And appearance. Mum, so much attention to the surface and approval; everybody's friend, agreeing, being nice. Nodding head when not really in accord, disguising and storing disapproval to relate to others whom she knew would agree. As for shame, the worst times for Sarah were the visits to the Free Trade Hall to hear the Halle Orchestra with a group from school, wearing her tailored coat which would have graced a fifty year old, and her school shoes. Her shame was always short-lived, evaporating in the music. She excelled at school and loved her uniform and white socks, her prefect's badge pinned to her tie.

Sarah experienced undreamed of luxury. Josie had gone and she had a room of her own. Her own room. Here she studied, dreamed and waited. And finally accepted that her mother had been blown to bits. Daniel and Sophie now talked little of Queenie but made self-consciously sure that she would be remembered. 'D'you remember when mum made your Cheshire Cat outfit for the school play?' 'Your mum always looked so smart in her black and white . . . .' Sarah loved their little references, locking up her own less favourable recollections. As did Sophie who had driven her daughter away at a time when she needed support, packed off in a cloud of lies, pregnant and by a Goy. This memory was pushed away whenever it surfaced. Daniel had not agreed to her arrangements for Queenie and Leonard to be away from the area yet had bowed to his wife's fierce determination.

Sarah was one of five to win a bursary to Manchester University and lived her student life with her grandparents, fearing for them, mindful of their increasing frailty. She was to wait until she was twenty before she moved out of the confines of Manchester. A period in France was a requirement for her degree. The prospect thrilled and frightened at the same time. Sophie chunnered, saw no need for it, all that palaver. Josie had gone and she didn't want her other granddaughter leaving home.

'Aren't you learning French at the university? Why d'you have to go abroad? It's such a lot of bother.'

Daniel quietly encouraged Sarah. He was so proud of her success at school.

Travel was not part of the family ethos. Sophie and Daniel had never had a holiday in their lives, bewildered by the concept. 'Packing a suitcase to schlepp on buses and trains, stay in someone else's house, a boarding house, eating strangers' food, wandering about in a strange town and paying good money for all that! Is that what we work so hard for?' Sophie made her perplexity clear: 'Oy, oy, oy!' A lament, a threnody, cathartic and dramatic, an outlet for Sophie's histrionic talent, a little parcel of scorn ornamented with eyes sliding right and upwards, and with downward intonation. 'Oy, oy, oy!' Josie and Sarah had once had a few days in a caravan in Cleveleys with their mother. The sea had entranced Sarah, and little else.

A train to London, a train to Paris with the channel ferry in between, and an overnight train to the South, to Perpignan, sleeping in a carriage with three strangers. Sarah was to know the irony of Salvador Dali's remark that Perpignan Station was the most beautiful station in the world, but she believed it to be so when she arrived. A small bus took her to her town on the outskirts of the city, her eyes gazing in wonder at the slope of the Eastern Pyrénées dropping down into the Mediterranean, the limestone Corbières, the heroic mountain, le Canigou, towering over this corner of France, 'La Montagne Sacrée des Catalans.' Sarah fell in love with Roussillon and the mountain.

Monsieur and Madame Delonca and their sturdy son welcomed her warmly to their home in a small ancient town, a hard working community largely indifferent to tourists and unselfconsciously aware of the domination of le Canigou and its range.

Journal 27 September:

I've been too overwhelmed even to write my journal. London, tickets, the Tube, another train; people so smart and slick I felt naïve, homespun and tense with the effort of trying to match them. I sat in the Tube next to folk falling asleep! I worked out that I would have to get off after three more stops and tried to look relaxed, faking sleep, even though I felt sick and frightened, out of my depth. I slept in a carriage from Paris to Perpignan on a top bunk, the other bunks being occupied by a Spanish family who offered me food. I had never had anchovies before. I hadn't thought to take food with me, my head being full of trains, vistas, the sea with no land in sight, my eyes stretched to their limits, everything unknown; I was a butterfly emerging from the safety of my chrysalis, programmed to open my wings and fly. I hope a grasping net will never descend on me.

I've never imagined (how could I?) living a life amongst mountains and plains, taking note of weather signs and moon phases; preparing a vegetable garden, a 'potager', according to whether the moon is waxing or waning; planting the bulbous vegetables like onions, garlic, beetroot at new moon and the leafy ones at full moon; a sine qua non. Vineyards spread over the plain and tuck into the mountainside like little bits of patchwork. Wine production determines the life of most families here making its varied demands the whole year round. My family, the Deloncas, contribute their produce to the local cooperative, living in the rhythms and counterpoint of the seasons and answering the demands of the vignobles; the sudden changes in the weather, the dramatic storms, ferocious in their short duration, clearing the sky for blue and sun. Apart from some technical improvements, (some would say, and often did, impediments) daily life is firmly shaped around the unexpected and the predictable, passions and acceptance, as it has been for generations. Uprooting has only to do with vines, vegetables and trees; not people. How different from my own forbears. These people have no need to adapt.

Sarah's few months in southern France passed all too quickly. Four days a week she took the bus into Perpignan for her courses, and around her studies lived a simple life, helping the family, learning how to cook, and adopting a broad southern accent.

Journal, May 15

My French now rolls, overflowing with sounds unsung in northern France. There is time here to expand words through their vowels.

I left this morning, all of us in tears, and promised to return. I'm still only halfway through France and already it's becoming dreamlike. How will I feel when I walk back into 103 Pendleton Street, into the drabness of sooty suburban streets? My eyes are narrowing, preparing their adjustment to cramped horizons, the separation from nature. I suppose I'll settle. Like sediment. Sophie and Daniel are happy there. Joseph and Mireille. And Jo and Jane will be getting married soon. Le Canigou, the magic mountain, has cast a spell on me. I will return, one day.

Chapter 6

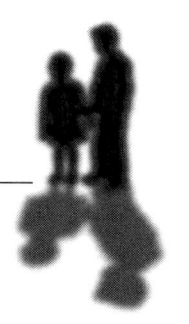

MORNING, AND ELEVEN PAIRS OF eyes fixed on the recumbent shape. It stirred, turned and sat up with a start. The eleven boys in Claude's new life were staring and smiling silently. They had been told of the possibility of the arrival of a new boy who may be frightened. They were to welcome him warmly, not to ask any questions, and Jean-Jacques Delmas in the next bed would take special care of him. Claude was bewildered by the silent smiling welcome. All these boys looking at him! He was struggling to remember where he was and what had happened. Why was nobody speaking? He was remembering now: the clock, oranges, banging of doors, 'we have done nothing wrong,' supper, cold and wasted, couldn't bend down, walking, 'don't run', the silver man, the funny ring, a fat man wiping his eyes. Where were they? Where were his parents and Rose? Were they here somewhere, going to surprise him? The young, slight Father Benedict swept into the dormitory, said a prayer, then the noise erupted. That was the rule; silence until after the prayer. The boys bellowed their hellos and bombarded Claude with questions, in spite of their instructions. Their curiosity was paramount. What time did you arrive? Where have you come from? Where are you parents? What have you brought with you? A flood of exuberance filled Claude's ears as he looked, wide-eyed, from one to the other of the high-spirited youngsters now gathered around his bed. He was at once stupefied and excited. Father Benedict eventually quietened the hubbub.

'Jean-Jacques will introduce our newcomer.'

Sitting on the next bed Jean-Jacques, to Claude's astonishment, told the boys his name was Jean-Pierre.

'No,' whispered Claude.

'He will be here until his parents return from America.' The boy continued ignoring Claude's small objection: 'No, they . . . .'

'We must not worry him with questions. His parents are a long way away.' Jean-Jacques had been well primed, knowing nothing of Claude's real life. Claude wondered for bewildering moments who the boy was talking about. It seemed it was him but he dared not contradict. Father Benedict hushed the burgeoning questions and bustled them all into their washing and dressing routines while he took charge of Claude to try to explain the need, just for a while, to pretend to be someone else; Jean-Pierre Bonnard. The boy was puzzled but silently accepted that to be a Jew at this time was dangerous. It had been a parsimonious explanation which he hadn't understood and he was too disturbed and timid to ask questions. He soon stopped asking 'Do you know where my parents are?' since repeatedly he heard 'No. You must try to put them out of your mind at present.' And 'We'll talk about that later.' And 'We don't know yet. You must fit in here for now.'

Jean-Jacques steered Claude through the following days of rituals, prayers, lessons, silences, manners, mass, confession. Claude stayed silent except for polite responses until he began to absorb his special lessons with Father Dominic. He felt as if he were playing a part in a dream, and not an unpleasant one. He liked his teacher, a plump, jolly man always ready to smile, his huge cassock not in the least intimidating. The part Claude learned loosened his tongue and gave free reign to his active imagination. Through his bewilderment a sense of exhilaration suffused his child's mind and body. His parents, he was sure, would come to get him soon. He began to quite enjoy the candles, the smell of incense, the sound of summoning bells, the company of the boys, the way every moment of the day was prescribed and safe. He genuflected and crossed himself with the grace of a dancer. He longed to dress in robes and regalia like some of the older boys. He soon came to chant Latin with the seriousness of a celebrant.

He fell into the life of the Pensionnat with surprising ease, enquiring less frequently about his family, simply accepting that no-one could answer his questions and he would just have to wait for them to come back. Meantime, the make-believe came fluently. He was ten years old and the lies which constructed a new past recreated Claude: Jean-Pierre Bonnard whose parents were in America on business and his sister with friends in Tours. When his mother and father come back they would collect their children and return to their life together in Paris. The story was so much more comfortable than having to tolerate uncertainty. 'I am Jean-Pierre Bonnard.'

Claude had been living in the Pensionnat for nearly a year now, the ritual life providing a family. The clock, the oranges, the sudden disappearance of his family were becoming faint memory traces. From the outset he learned his new lines well, encouraged ardently by the Fathers.

'I am Jean-Pierre Bonnard. My father is Jean Christian Bonnard, my mother is called Jeanne after Jeanne d'Arc. My sister whose name is Thérèse is in Tours. All my relatives live in America. My parents will be returning for me as soon as they have finished their business there. Their business is to do with wine. I don't know more than that.' 'I don't know' was to be the response to any question outside their script that someone may ask. Claude wondered who it was would be asking the questions. The one question, 'Are you a Jew?' he had to be sure to get perfectly right in his answer: 'My family are Catholics. That's why I am here.' Father Dominic worked hard with Claude, asking questions, rehearsing replies in training for the day when some people may come to the school and interrogate him. It seemed people did that these days. Claude knew by now that these people were Germans who had taken over their country. Father Dominic's earnestness came through his jolly exterior conveying to Claude the urgency of learning his part well even though the boy did not understand why. Nor did he question. There was some part of his mind which was attending to reconciling what had been irreconcilable by removing the offending bits of history and replacing them with a more tolerable story. His new forged Carte d'Identité in the name of Jean-Pierre Bonnard authenticated his replaced past.

'Jean-Pierre' delighted in telling his fellow pupils of his parents' life in America where everyone was rich. Of course, he didn't receive food parcels because America was too far away. The cake would be mouldy and the jars of honey would break on the journey.

'In America, did you know you can eat chicken and fishcakes every day? There are bowls of olives on every table. And they have so much fruit and cake some of it goes rotten before they have time to eat it. You can eat herrings whenever you like.'

Father Dominic had done a splendid job of teaching his pupil to lie. He struggled bitterly with his conscience. The staff knew of the interest the Germans took in schools, searching, questioning, inspecting papers, suspicious of everyone, diligent in their task to ferret out hidden Jewish children, following the expediency of destroying vermin before it can reproduce.

Lying was a sin at the Pensionnat but Claude learned that it didn't really matter because he could confess at appointed times and be absolved, which he took to mean 'let off'. He enjoyed the notion that, no-matter what he did, he would be sent away to say some incomprehensible phrases a number of times, specified by the priest. He had been taught to say a rigmarole which began 'Father, I have sinned . . .'. He had to invent some sins. One could not go to confession sinless even though he felt he was. Everyone sins every day and night he was told. He did envy the food parcels the other pupils received. So as to really sin he stole from the kitchen, only a small amount, out of each private store. He decided for himself that all the honey, cakes and jam which most pupils received, labelled and stored covetously in the large kitchen cupboard, should be shared, even if the owners knew nothing of their generosity. He would confess his sins altogether, later.

The boy Alfred Schumacher was a less tractable pupil for Father Dominic. Months ago Alfred had returned from Paris from a weekend visit to his aunt in Melun to find no-one at the station to meet him. It was 7.30pm. He knew the way home and set off, alone and puzzled, through the dark streets. He had never been allowed to be out alone after dark. Perhaps they thought he was now, at nine years old, grown up enough to make his own way home. He took a bus then walked for half an hour to arrive at his family's dress shop to find it in complete darkness, the front door locked and no sign of his parents and his elder brother, Elie, to welcome him. A neighbour was looking out for him, an elderly lady who knew the family well. She took him by the arm and steered him down the street away from his house, explaining that they had all had to go away unexpectedly. In the mean time he would stay in a new place, a school where he would be well looked after. The brave Fathers at the Pensionnat hastily greeted Madame Castel; they clearly knew her from other courageous deeds and they took him in. Ever since, he had been in a state of shock, scarcely uttering a word to anyone, obediently doing as he was asked, politely monosyllabic. Father Dominic tried to explain that he would have to have a new name, a new story and a new identity card. It would be of great help to him in the future and Alfred would have to trust his word. Alfred nodded, habitually courteous, but quite unable to pronounce his invented name, Alain Soler; 'my name is Alain Soler. I am an orphan,' let alone the rest of the story. He clung resolutely to his own name and the memories locked inside his silence, his world elsewhere. The Father could make no inroads.

A day soon came when the grandfather clock, the oranges, the gleaming shop, the abandoned Sabbath Eve supper pierced the thin fabric of Claude's cover. His dormitory was quiet, children were asleep or nearly so when the fisted thumping on the front door of the school slammed into their ears. Harsh voices, aggressive footsteps, the scurrying light footsteps of the Fathers brought a flash of the past into Claude's head.

Father Michel opened the large oak front door.

'TAKE US TO ALFRED SCHUMACHER!' Two men for one small child. Father Michel talked to them as they pushed in, asserting that, to his knowledge, there was no-one in the school by that name. He played for time. Father Dominic discreetly left the group in the hall and, once out of sight, ran up the stairs to the dormitory. On the way he thanked God they had not asked for Claude Blum. All the boys were sitting up, frightened by the brutally disturbing sounds. The Father whispered to Claude to stay silent as he quickly passed his bed and went to sit beside Alfred, gripping his tiny hands. He was panting with exertion and fear.

'You *must* remember, you must say, my name is Alain Soler, my name is Alain Soler, Alain Soler. I am an orphan. Say it! Say, my name is Alain Soler! Please say it!' The children had never seen their teacher in such an agitated state, almost angry, squeezing the child's hands too tightly. Every pupil willed the boy to repeat the words, knowing intuitively that it was a matter of great urgency. Alfred was scared and tried:

' . . . my name is Alain . . . Alfred. Alain Schumacher. Alfred Schumacher. My name is Alfred Schumacher.'

'God help the child.' Father Dominic crossed himself and moved towards the door just as two men burst in with Father Michel. A man in a long overcoat pushed past the Father as he opened the door.

'EVERY CHILD STAND UP!' This person knew that his victim was here. The children stood stiffly by their beds.

'Raise your hand ALFRED SCHUMACHER!' The two fathers silently prayed. The children willed Alfred to do nothing. Alfred raised his hand. The overcoated man smiled as the officer in SS uniform strutted across the aisle and stood looking down on the trembling child. Claude saw only the two thin white legs and small bare feet opposed to the brilliant shine of long hard leather boots. The aggression of the uniform and overcoat was like a discordant counterpoint against the white feet and nightshirts of the boys and the robes of the Fathers.

Alfred was scooped up.

'He's wet through with pee, this little Jew-boy,' the uniformed man bellowed, laughing. Alfred Schumacher in his nightshirt was carried out, as inert as a dead body, as if he knew his fate.

'You, too, will come with us.' A finger jabbed into the chest of Father Michel. Head bowed, knowing there was no point in resisting, he walked on with them, a silent step alongside their hideous clacking heels. The entrance door to the Pensionnat slammed behind them. Father Dominic knelt down just where he was, praying, waiting for the discipline of prayer to dispel his anger, to assuage his impotence to help the child and his beloved colleague, to quell his outrage, his curses and, worst of all, the shame of being thankful it had been Alfred and not Claude. There was not enough time now. He would hope to find consolation and compassion later after he had calmed and reassured those now in his charge. There were a few moments of doubt. He had them infrequently but powerfully. In these moments he was aware of the cunning game of pick and choose at which the mind excels, the duplicitous escape routes clearing the pathway of guilt and conflict. The elderly Father's route was via the Catholic faith; usually he was quickly restored through his prayers

The children were told to take a blanket from their beds and find their places in the chapel. They prayed fervently for the two departed members of their family. Most of them did not understand what was happening, except they knew it was terrible. There were those who knew, aside from a miracle, they would never see Father Michel or Alfred Schumacher again. Tears flowed freely, some boys rocked themselves, others were statue still; teachers clamped their teeth together in an attempt to seem strong in front of their pupils, to find the self-restraint they had so often practised. Claude Blum's memories appeared again, now vivid and stirring. The thumping on the front door filled his head. His body was gripped by fear. He knew Jean-Pierre Bonnard was make-believe and that something terrible may have happened to his family. Next time they may come for him. He would be ready and strong. That's what papa had meant.

For all Father Dominic's kindness, care and competence, they all missed the serene soul of Father Michel. They missed the quiet secretive presence of Alfred Schumacher. As a matter of course pupils and staff departed from the Pensionnat from time to time to pursue new, chosen lives. But now two of their community had been prised away by forceful leather-gloved hands and pushed into an unknown, scarcely imaginable future. 'Working for Germany.' Father Michel was seventy years old, Alfred was nine. They would all know sooner or later that those over sixty years old and children were considered ill-fit for work and therefore disposable.

In the following evenings, after the children had been settled into their beds, tasks accomplished, their familiarity giving solace, the Fathers talked quietly together. They had been complicit in sheltering Alfred; the powers in the land may well return, and the school had Claude Blum in its midst.

'We are in danger,' Father Benedict declared. It had been two days since the departure of Alfred and Father Michel. After many prayers it was time to decide. It was time to address the practical. Father Benedict, the youngest teacher, faced his colleagues with a clear-eyed, sober view of their circumstances.

'Let's not delude ourselves, my dear friends. We have harboured a Jewish child. We are therefore culpable in the eyes of those who now rule this country. And . . .' He faltered and swallowed hard. 'We have to face the facts. There are French people who are ready to assist the Occupiers in their evil intent to be rid of the Jews. We can't hide behind our faith. You cannot have helped but see the hideous hoardings posted around our city. The Jew, ringleted, swarthy, with a huge nose and thick leering lips, suspended on puppet strings by the blond Aryan master. Evil is all around us.'

'How d'you seem to know so much?' asked Monsieur Conte, a lay member of the teaching staff. Father Benedict hesitated before responding.

'I am a member of a 'réseau'. It's an organisation. To rid us of the evil in our midst. I can say no more than that.'

Father Dominic knew of his fellow priest's courageous underground work and felt a great love for him.

'Yes, my dear friend Benedict, you are right. We must close the school and transfer our children to other schools. And then remove ourselves to safer places. We need to work quickly now.'

They were all well aware of the special interest the SS had in schools, always searching, inspecting identity cards, asking children their names, looking under beds and in cupboards. 'Where are your parents? Do you have a brother or sister? Where are they?' They were zealous in their task to root out hidden Jewish children. Monsieur Conte asked, 'And what of Claude Blum?'

'Yes, what about Claude Blum?' Father Benedict rubbed his forehead. 'I have friends who live in Blois. They will take him and make arrangements for him one way or another. He has relations in Marseille. These friends are trustworthy and do what they can. The best we can do is just get him there. And then our duty is done. Trust me, dear friends. But we must act now, before a return visit.'

Father Dominic left the group, heavy with grief, to pray for the wisdom to do the best thing for everyone and to start the preparations for the children.

He was spared making preparations for most of the children. A practical, peremptory sequence of events took the responsibility out of his hands. As the news of the two departures spread, parents, or relations in loco parentis, began to arrive to remove their children from the Pensionnat. They were bewildered by the removal of the head of the school and a pupil but the smell of danger hurried them away from the school, asking few questions. After a matter of two weeks there remained only four boys out of thirty, two whose parents hadn't yet heard, one whose parents and family were abroad, and Claude. The three boys were seen safely on their way, two reunited with their parents and the other with his grandmother in Vincenne, leaving Claude mystified and lonely. The Fathers kept him busy helping them to clean and tidy the school, an essential dutiful act however rapidly performed, ready for closure and departure, to wait to be filled again after the madness was over. And meantime Father Benedict could make his arrangements.

Claude, for all his confusion, threw himself into the tasks he was given, feeling useful and important. He was yet to realise just how central his presence had been to the upheaval. But he felt the vibrations of urgency and fearfulness. Their German visitors may return.

Father Benedict had contacted a member of his network to enlist help to transport Claude and Father Dominic, who insisted on going with him, to Blois. It was judged to be a temporary safe haven for the child. Blois was just inside the occupied zone. At this stage, at this time, it would be too risky to try to take Claude across the line into the so-called Free Zone. All the roads and stations were heavily guarded along the line from Biarritz, through Bordeaux, Angouleme, Tours and across France to the Swiss border at Geneva. And anyway Father Benedict explained to his colleagues that trains of 'deportees' were leaving the 'Free' Zone headed ultimately for the camps. There had been many eyewitness accounts of such evacuations. He made it plain that the Free Zone was not free; that the Vichy government was simply a puppet, doing the work of the Occupiers; that Jews were not now safe anywhere in France and elsewhere. He urged the staff to forgive their fellow French for their complicity, their timidity, for whatever motive drove them in an occupied defeated nation. He selected his words and told them nothing of the enthusiasm of the French Milicia; of his belief it was a time when unexpressed, and for some, unconscious, racism could legitimately be revealed, or dredged up, and acted upon all the more fiercely, with permission.

The school spick and span, prayers said, farewells all made, they were ready, the last of them to leave; two priests and a child. There remained one more task; to remind Claude of his origins, his family, his Jewish heritage. And emphasise why he had been given a new identity. If the need were to arise he could still play his part. Father Benedict busied himself with the finishing touches inside the school. The car was due in an hour. Claude and Father Dominic sat in the small garden at the back of the school under the plane tree on whose patchy bark many initials had been illicitly carved, a tiny CB to be found at the base of the trunk. Claude had talked to his teacher about his lightning flashes of memory, always wondering if they were really memories or make-believe. Neither had edges. Like most young children he easily tolerated the uncertain merging of real and imaginary. He knew his mother and father and Rose were real, he felt them so vigorously inside himself. They were palpable, appearing for fleeting moments in different places, delicately absorbed; Rose sitting alert, involved, fingering the keys of the piano, playing a little Mozart minuet; Papa bent over his bench, meticulously repairing a watch with tiny gold screwdrivers; maman laughing, teasing him as she dextrously filleted a fish. Snapshots randomly presented, lucid, untidy details in the wink of an eye; the glittering shop in twilight, black olives in a dark blue bowl, candle flames dancing. And the feelings, sounds and smells that came and went, elusive sensory moments; the soft touch of Lili's caress rubbing a hand through his bristly hair, stroking his thin back as he sat on her knee; the aroma of supper on the table, the murmur of traffic on the street, a scent of candle wax; the feel of wood under fingertips, the smell of oranges, his small hand inside the soft warmth of his father's as they walked together.

'Jean-Pierre.' Father Dominic corrected himself. 'No, I mean Claude. My dear child, Claude. There are things I have to tell you.' He cleared his throat. 'There are good forces and evil forces in the world. In each of us. We have both of us done and thought wicked things. Sometimes wickedness seems to triumph over good.' Claude remembered the food he had stolen and braced himself for his comeuppance. The elderly Father shifted about on the bench. He had carefully prepared his account. It was to have been subtle, philosophical, historical, about forgiveness, compassion and grace. He looked at the small child next to him and silently wept.

'They know not what they do!' he blurted out, abandoning his script. 'You are a Jew! Jewish! You are in danger. Always in danger. Jews are constantly in danger. Now the Germans want to be rid of all Jews. You need to know that. And don't ask me why. I don't know.' He cradled his head in his hands. Claude had never seen a grown-up really crying. He had seen tears in grown-ups' eyes, often not knowing why they were there, and especially puzzled when tears shone at times of pleasure; sharing Friday night supper with their closest friends, taking plaited loaves out of the oven, watching Guignol in the park. But only children really cry. He looked up into the Father's sad face.

'I'll be alright,' he said in a quiet voice. 'Don't worry, you'll see. I know I'm a Jew. I've always known that. Even Jean-Pierre Bonnard knew. Please don't cry. My father told us that our great grandfather was a Jewish émigré. He came to France, you know, because it was dangerous in his own country. Families were often separated, papa said. Now we're in danger in our own country, and we are apart. And I don't know why some people used to shout 'Jopins!' after us when we lived on Avenue Louis Blanc. It's a rude name for Jew, you know. My parents told me we would have our own country one day. Goy is a rude word, too, for Gentile. I expect you know it. I heard the older boys say that the war was about Jews. One day we'll be in our own home, you'll see. And you can come and visit us there. We'll make a great feast for you in our country. We won't be in danger there, Benjamin told me. He said, 'Jews will soon have their rightful place.' He told me to hold those words in my heart.' The old priest knew it was he who was being comforted. He could not remember who said 'the child is father of the man'. The words rang in his ears. He understood something new and had nothing more to say. The two smiled at each other and left the garden for the last time.

The car had arrived punctually. The driver was called 'Mercure' they were told as they put their two small cases in the boot. They were also told he would not want to talk on the journey. As the two settled themselves on the back seat Mercure turned round and smiled warmly at each of them, giving the boy a knowing wink, a reassuring connection. They departed, young Father Benedict assuring them they were safe and giving them his blessing. They would learn later that the young priest had been picked up by the Gestapo, questioned, tortured and deported for his involvement with the Resistance.

The two passengers, accustomed to silence, understood in their own way the need for it. The priest's eyes stared ahead seeing nothing. Claude feasted his eyes on the changing landscape, questions burning but committed to silence, a discipline he had grown used to. Three hours later the car came to a halt in front of a small double-fronted detached, lace-curtained house on the outskirts of Blois. Madame Carmet appeared at the front door. She had been watching out for their arrival. Claude saw a neat diminutive figure, grey haired, smiling, hands anxiously clasped, wearing a floral wrap-around pinafore. The thought tugged at Claude: 'She looks nothing like my mother. She may not like me.' The priest and the child scurried across the pavement from the car into a narrow hallway, ushered in with warm words and furtive glances up and down the street. The car moved off quickly without a word from Mercure. They were led into the comforting warmth and aromas of the kitchen on the right of the little hallway. The square deal table was set for three and something cooking smelled of care and attentiveness, evoking in Claude traces of memory from Avenue Louis Blanc. It was pot-au-feu, a dish he loved.

Madame Carmet put Claude's small case on the first step of the stairs then chattily seated them at the table. They both made appreciative noises as she served them her excellent stew, an incomparable welcome. The pleasantries and the meal over the old man explained: 'Claude. You will hide here until such time as you will be taken to a safe place. We will try to get you to Marseille to your grandmother and uncle with whom we have been in touch. In the meantime you must stay quiet and unnoticed. Madame Carmet has made arrangements for you to be here, unobserved and safe until . . .' He cleared his throat several times, a sign of his uncertainty. 'Until you will be amongst loved ones.' Claude had last seen his maternal grandmother and her son, Thierry, his uncle, years ago just before the start of the war after which it had become impossible for them to meet, to the great sadness of his mother, indeed of all the family.

They had regularly spent time all together years ago. Claude could scarcely remember them.

'I don't suppose my mother and father and Rose be there, will they?' Seeing the distress on the face of the priest Madame Carmet intervened.

'Who knows anything, my dear child? Maybe, maybe not. But the important thing is that we now say goodbye to our dear friend and settle you in here.'

'I will be staying nearby, Claude. I will come and see you soon. God bless.' He took his leave quickly, whispering a few words to Madame Carmet as he departed. Claude felt reassured by the elderly lady. She settled him in to his little bedroom overlooking her back garden full of tidy rows of vegetables and a few fruit trees on the edges. Beyond the garden as far as the eye could see were hectares of vines now black and stunted at this time of the year, looking as though they could never be fruitful again. Claude would watch them burgeon whilst waiting.

Madame Carmet had been advised to keep Claude at home, away from the curious neighbours. She was not convinced that her story was accepted that he was here on a short holiday after an illness, she being an old friend of the family. Claude, then, was almost entirely confined to the house and garden. He found it difficult, tedious and bewildering. Why were there so many lies, why was he made to tell them, what was it that made it dangerous to be a Jew, where were maman and papa and Rose? And when would he have to move on again down to Marseille to stay with his grandmother and uncle Thierry whom he could scarcely remember, if at all? Would maman and papa and Rose be there when he arrived?

'Madame, if my parents and Rose aren't going to be there in Marseille where exactly will they be?'

Madame Carmet had been asked this question several times since Claude's arrival and the lies continued.

'We don't know where they are, I've told you. But you'll be with family.' It was Claude's confusion that troubled her most.

'But if I go back to being Jean-Pierre Bonnard they could be in America on business and coming back to pick me up. Do they know our address? Will you tell them your address, Madame?'

Madame Carmet feared for this small boy who now seemed unable to separate fact from fiction. His new identity had probably saved his life but at what cost? She would talk to Father Dominic when he visited. The boy's bewilderment and perhaps lack of the company of boys of his own age pushed him into silence. He was always polite and helpful but had stopped asking when he would be leaving and where his parents and sister were, and what was so wrong about being a Jew. Madame Carmet explained to Father Dominic that he seemed to have gone into a world of his own, that he often smiled dreamily. He was becoming unreachable. The two adults worried and Father Dominic tried to hasten Claude's departure hoping that being with loving family would restore him. Madame was concerned that he was so quiet and introvert because he had no companions of his age but she could not risk letting him go out to play with the local children. She knew it would be only a few weeks until plans were made to get him down to Marseille.

Claude made up his mind that he didn't really like Jean-Pierre Bonnard and would push him away whenever he tried to take over. He would speak to him quietly for fear that Madame Carmet may hear.

'You can just go away, Jean-Pierre Bonnard. You lie and you take me away from my family. Get out of my head. I want to be with Rose and my parents now. And I don't want to be a Catholic and pretend I'm not a Jew. I don't want to keep repeating all that Latin stuff. You don't have Friday night suppers which I'll have soon with the others. I wonder where they are, they'll come back for me, you'll see. I'll keep asking them to. And we don't need incense and the body and blood of Christ and all that. And you can bugger off.' He was quite pleased with his swearing and kept repeating 'bugger off, bugger off' with evident satisfaction.

Claude found that the best way to get rid of Jean-Pierre Bonnard was to take himself into his father's shop and look at all the shiny-ness of all the clocks and jewellery. Or to the kitchen to find out what maman was cooking. Or to visit the patisserie-boulangerie opposite to buy a baguette and occasionally four little glazed fruit tarts.

Madame Carmet was greatly relieved when the arrangements were made and Father Martin arrived to accompany Claude on his journey south.

Chapter 7

CLAUDE ARRIVED AT THE STATION in Marseille accompanied by Father Dominic's friend, the elderly but spry Father Martin, and took a bus to his grandmother's home in the sprawling suburbs. They stood on the doorstep of her neat little house in a shaded, unremarkable street, Claude clutching his scuffed, mock-leather suitcase. Father Martin knocked gently on the door. A tiny silver haired head peeped round the fractionally opened door, dark eyes glinting. Claude had rehearsed: 'I am your grandson, Claude. You haven't seen me for a long time, you probably won't recognise me . . . .' He needn't have rehearsed his speech.

'Claude!' She opened the door wide and embraced him with a force which crushed and warmed him. Father Martin stayed only a few moments in the hallway to explain that, for the sole purpose of enabling the journey to Marseille, Claude's papers showed him to be his noviciate on his way to the Catholic collegiate in Marseille. They had been lucky. There had been a commotion at the border into the free zone. The station platform had been more than usually packed, people jostling, shouting, an elderly couple searching nervously for their papers to show an official, a young man pushing through the crowd pursued by a policeman, an atmosphere of impending chaos. They had gone by unchecked.

Claude was swept by his tiny black clad grandmother, Mamie Alice, into the hub of the house, the kitchen. A half familiar figure was standing by the cast iron stove.

'Your uncle Thierry!' Claude just remembered the quiet, shy young brother of his mother from the days when they used to get together for family occasions. Thierry looked nothing like his sister; Claude was disappointed to find nothing about his Uncle Thierry which might resemble his mother. He was reserved, very thin and blond, in entire contrast to her. Thierry embraced him warmly. Father Martin left hastily, his job done. He was thanked profusely for delivering his charge safely and sent on his way with a tin of iced chestnuts. Claude could see only vestiges of his fair, youthful uncle. He looked nearly old, hardly recognisable. Thierry and Mamie fussed over the preparation of a bouillabaisse, asking Claude if he liked this or that. Did he like conger eel, rouille, fennel, monk fish, rascasse? Claude had never eaten this dish so beloved of the Marseillais, full of fish fresh from their bay. He nodded politely to all their enquiries thinking how quickly they talked and with such a strong accent. Then the aroma filled his nose exquisitely as he watched them from his chair at the table, anticipating their special way of welcoming him. The kitchen was shabby, not like his mother's, with cracked geometric tiles on the floor, an ill-fitting lace curtain at the window, an old dresser looking drunk as it leaned to the left, weighed down with with pots, pans, crockery. 'I didn't know they were poor,' Claude thought. 'They don't even have a proper tablecloth,' he observed, staring at the yellow floral oilcloth on the table. He was shocked to find how small his bedroom was. A huge mahogany set of drawers dwarfed the tiny bed. And there was nothing else in the room. His own room in Avenue Louis Blanc had a huge bed, drawers, wardrobe, table for writing and drawing and some shelves for his books and school work. This was terrible but he would be back soon he told himself and was comforted by the thought.

Mamie bossed Thierry, her six foot plus son, but good-naturedly. They dined warmly, chatting about the food, the journey with Father Martin, the Pensionnat, though it was quite difficult to get this diffident young boy to talk. The habit of being Jean-Pierre Bonnard still had a strong hold over him. The fear of 'letting slip' at the Pensionnat at a wrong moment, the confusion of this huge lie, the return to being Claude in the garden with Father Dominic, and then being a student of a priest for the journey to Marseille all filled his head with turmoil, uncertainty and fear. Saying little seemed safest.

Alice spoke and moved very rapidly compared to Thierry's slow, calm demeanour. Claude was polite and reticent. They listened to Claude's story unfolding bit by bit as the time passed, silently filling in the unexplained puzzling parts. Claude was slow to tell these people he scarcely knew of his experiences, standing in the grandfather clock up to his arrival at their home. He told his story as if he were describing someone else. Thierry and Alice never pushed him, waiting patiently for the moments when he seemed ready to talk. Claude would spurt out disjointed bits of his life at unexpected times, just before going to bed, in the middle of doing his homework, on a walk with his grandmother to the market. It was difficult at first for them to piece together a coherent picture of what he had been through, though the horror of it all for this young boy was evident in all he said. There was not an iota of self-pity in his chilling narrative. Thierry and Mamie shared their anxiety about the effects this experience might have on Claude's state of mind.

Thierry had heard through his contacts of the abrupt disappearance of his sister Lily, her husband David and his niece Rose. He knew of the dawn raids, 'les rafles', the Germans were making on Jewish homes in Paris and elsewhere. It was not enough to vilify Jews, exclude them, strip them of jobs and dignity but now they had to be 'removed'. Due to the sacrifice and bravery of others, and for some the sacrifice of their lives, he could rejoice in the presence of his nephew, here, in relative safety. Since nothing was certain these days he had decided to keep his information to himself until he could find out more. When he had learnt of Claude's imminent arrival in Marseille he had to tell his mother what he had heard. Madame Levine received the news of the probable fate of her daughter and family the day before her grandson appeared on her doorstep. She said, quite simply, 'I will take care of my grandson as best I can. Even though I am dead inside.' At this moment she found herself unable to cry.

Alice, whose life had been simple and mostly happy could scarcely even conceive of what had happened to her family. Thierry had tried to soften the telling by leaving out some of the details he had heard about the deportations and their sequels. Alice was not fooled.

She had been brought up in an area close to the port, the daughter of Jewish folk who had lived in France for generations as far as they knew and who celebrated their faith only on those special days of the Jewish calendar. It was of little significance to them or to their friends and neighbours that they were not Catholic like most people around them. What mattered was to make a living, help one's neighbours and bring up the children in a healthy and respectable way. Her father had been an astute market trader highly respected for the quality of his produce. They kept chickens, rabbits and a goat and were proudly self-sufficient. Her mother's life centred on her family, the animals, the produce, bottling and preserving according to the seasons; beautiful skills which Alice learnt and loved and always wore lightly. At a young age she could 'prick out' the tomatoes, milk the goat, plant the melon seeds, find the elusive chanterelle mushrooms, pluck a chicken. She couldn't wait to leave school, which she enjoyed and did well. But her heart was with the family and the seasonal challenges in all their forms.

Alice and her brother Thomas took over the potager when the parents got older and Alice ran it single-handedly when her brother went to war in 1914, never to be seen again. Her life was badly shaken by this event but she was young and healthy and found a man she loved. She was utterly determined that her two children, Lily and Thierry, would be educated, better themselves, but stay attached to the rhythms and beauty of her world. She felt certain that they would never have to endure a war like the one she had lived through. She knew and heard of so many young men who had been 'killed in battle', who had 'sacrificed their lives for their country' in what was extraordinarily called 'The Great War'.

And now, the madness of another war in which not just young men went to the slaughter but whole families of Jews. 'Why Jews?' she would often ask her son, with a slow uncomprehending shake of the head. 'Why, Thierry? Tell me, what did we do, we Jews?' but not expecting any kind of explanation nor receiving one. After the invasion of her country, the occupation, she had feared every waking moment for her daughter, Lily, in Paris whose stubborn husband, David would not budge an inch out of Paris in spite of having two young children. She had feared every waking moment for her son, Thierry who sent covert messages to her to let her know he was safe in whatever dangerous circumstance he worked. His whereabouts were never known to her, only that he was part of the Maquis and the likelihood of being caught was high.

Alice dug her heels in when Thierry began to talk about moving to a safer place as it became clear that the 'free zone' was increasingly occupied by the Germans after the Americans entered the war.

'I will never leave this place. You go and take young Claude with you. But I will not move.' Her voice was unusually strident. 'This is my home, I've been here for over forty years and no Germans are going to force me out!'

'Mother, listen to me,' Thierry pleaded in his slow, soft way. 'You are being as stubborn as David and look what happened to them. I'll find a safer place, I know a lot of people further south. Marseille isn't safe now. At least just consider it. They've been blowing up parts of the old town round the port and they need the port in case of an invasion from this part of the Med.' He knew that Marseille old town had recently been dynamited in a massive clearance project aimed to reduce opportunities for resistance members to hide and operate in the densely populated old buildings known to the Germans as 'terrorists' nests', facts which Thierry had played down in the telling to his mother. She knew something terrible had happened when most of the lights went out around the port.

'You should go, and take my grandson.' Thierry heard the fear behind her words.

'You don't really expect me to take off with Claude and leave you here.' Thierry knew he had a serious decision to make, firm in the knowledge that his mother would never move out of their house unless forced and that he could not do. She had become very silent after her acceptance of the fate of her family and now even more so after hearing of the destruction of the old town she knew so well. When her son encouraged her to talk she explained, quite simply and quietly, that her light had gone out too.

Should he take the boy to a safer place, leave him and return to Marseille? Indeed, where was this place? It was common knowledge that the Germans were now everywhere including small villages, rooting out resistance workers and encouraging 'collabos'. Perhaps a busy city was as safe a place as any. And given there was a good deal of hunger amongst French people he knew he would always be able to find food for them. What was increasingly worrying for Thierry were the rumours of the disappearance of Jews from all parts of Europe, the French Jews from the South being sent to Fréjus, from there to Compiègne, then Drancy internment camp to board trains to concentration camps God knew where.

Alice had had serious misgivings about the decision her daughter and son-in-law had made to stay in Paris, steeling herself daily for news from her son of what was happening there. It had been hard and dreadful to be cut off from them since the Occupation; no visits, few letters, only snatches of news through her son's underground links. She had coped with her fear by busying herself with tasks which still gave her pleasure; she bottled fruit and vegetables from her potager at the back of the house and sold some of her preserves and fresh produce on the local market; she loved the seasonal changes yielding early garlic, young lettuces and radishes and parsley through to the glut of peaches, nectarines, apricots, plums and onto olives, autumn apples, quinces, chard. No-one knew better how to deal with an abundance of winter cabbages and leeks. No-one knew better how to preserve mushrooms. There was a very old and prized medlar tree in the corner of her garden and no-one knew better how to make delicious jam and paste from its small orange fruits. Now she knew she would never again be able to take comfort in the rhythms that had sustained her.

Thierry knew for sure that the family had perished and he vowed to himself that he would one day get this boy, Claude, to England where he would be with members of his family who had fled from France. He still anticipated reprisals for his part in the network and so feared for the boy. But it would not be prudent to try and move him at the present time.

Claude found security with his maternal grandmother, Alice, whom he called Mamie, and his uncle Thierry. The lad was quiet, withdrawn. Their memory of him before the enforced separation of the family after the occupation was very different; a chatty, confident child, liking the centre stage, overshadowing his shy, diffident sister with his sunny disposition. 'What d'you expect after all he's gone through?' Alice reasoned. 'Shut up in a clock case for all that time, listening to God knows who taking his family to God knows where. And then wandering the streets to the Catholic school. And having to pretend to be someone else!' Alice was getting distressed and, in spite of Thierry's arms around her urging her to be calm, continued. 'And then he had to travel the length of the country, Germans at every turn . . . .' Her thin frame shook inside Thierry's arms.

'He's just a child, Thierry. No child should have to go through that. He's quiet, yes, what d'you expect? Heaven only knows what this'll do to him in the future.' They wept together. Going round and round in Thierry's head was something he had heard—that many of them did not die quickly. And now, a Jew is a Jew, first and foremost, irrespective of his country, and a solution, a final solution, to the 'Jewish problem' had been agreed upon at the highest level

Claude's occasionally expressed hopes and wonderings about his parents and Rose were damped down by Alice's downcast eyes, the almost imperceptible shake of Thierry's head and briefly exchanged glances; questions shrugged off with comforting blandness. 'We'll have to wait and see.' 'We don't know anything for sure.' And an abrupt change of subject.

The war began to come to an end and Claude settled quickly into his new home with its reassuring routines. The irrefutable facts of the deportations and the camps were beginning to be uncovered and Claude felt the truth painfully winding its way into his mind. It dawned on him what the lowered eyelids and quick glances had meant. One evening, at supper, Claude announced, 'They're dead. My parents and Rose. In the camps.' He was not asking but stating. There was no need for, nor was there a response. The little family finished their bowls of soup in desolate silence, indifferent to the remaining half-full tureen and dish of croutons a l'ail in the centre of the table, all lovingly prepared and for once disregarded. Claude felt strangely cold and impassive. The war was all but over and the truth was emerging. He knew cold facts but no part of him could accommodate the utter horror of the fate of his family. Papa, maman and Rose would stay alive inside him. He would never let them die.

As they always did, Claude and Thierry thanked Alice for their supper and each went their separate heavy ways to habitual niches in the kitchen, Claude to his homework on the little card table by the range, Thierry to his wicker chair opposite, always papers and lists to check for the restaurant he had re-established, and Alice to clear up after the half-eaten meal and then to bed. Claude stared down at his books seeing images tumbling one on top of the other; the glinting magic of the shop, his father, impeccably dressed, enjoying the contact with his customers, sensitive to their wishes, the bonhomie with friends who dropped in for a gossip, the dusting and polishing, the table set for supper, his mother's embrace when he came home from school, his casse-croute, the little snack waiting for him, often a portion of baguette with a square of dark chocolate, Rose wanting help with her homework, the hum of traffic on the avenue, people rushing home. Home.

These were not memories. 'May I have some more chicken, maman? I was third in maths today. Did you know there are squirrels that can fly? They have parachutes on their backs.' Claude's future was now irrevocably displaced by his life and breath in Avenue Louis Blanc.

As Alice bade them goodnight Claude, looking up from his books, his kaleidoscope, saw how tiny and careworn she was, her skin transparent and her clothes loose on her frail body. He had never dared ask why she was always dressed in black. He could not imagine her being young and full of vitality like his mother. In that sudden instant, behind his small smile and his 'Dors bien, Mamie,' he knew she would soon be gone, someone else disappearing out of his life. She would stay alive in his head, like the rest of the family

Alice died in her sleep three days later, at last spared from her numbing grief. Thierry seemed spared, too, deep down within his sorrow. After her burial he began to feel free to tell his nephew a little of his life in Bordeaux, before he had taken refuge with his mother, when he was part of a network, 'un réseau', in the early stages of the war, a group which had set about subversive activities to undermine the German occupation of their country.

His tongue loosed: 'My section's focus was to disrupt any form of communication from railways to telephone lines. And my particular job was to search out and organise escape routes into Spain. We had started as a tiny, dedicated group which grew into a powerful network in a matter of a year. You know Claude, the Gestapo, with the help of 'collabos', the bastards who gave us away, tortured and, if they were not already dead, deported a lot of our members. All in good time you'll hear about the infamous Fort du Ha in Bordeaux where they committed their atrocities, when more of the truth of this terrible time in our lives comes out. I don't think people will believe the half of it. Many brave men and women died; horribly.' Claude listened, silent, enthralled. 'I managed to leave Bordeaux when I knew they were hot on my heels, at the point when very little was left of our network. God knows, I urged the remaining members to do the same before yet another of us was denounced. Six of them, five men and a woman stayed on. I don't know if they were heroic or just plain bloody-minded but none of them survived. One was my dear friend, Adeline. Her code name was Hirondelle.' Thierry clenched his teeth through a long silence, attempting to keep control of his emotions. He was sparing of the details, bursting with pride for his friends and compatriots with whom he had worked. Claude was fascinated, and removed from any connection there may be to the fate of his family. He loved the code names of the members of the network: Lys, Poulet,

Jacot, Dekobra, Hirondelle, Aramis, Mamie, La Gazelle, Vautour, le Docteur, l'Ingenieur, Chappelle. Thierry gave each the weight of his respect. 'All so different, from different backgrounds. some of them were out and out criminals, others from bourgeois families, and working class folk like me. And, oh, so many more. Nearly all tortured and deported. Many 'mort en déportation'. The network was finally broken and, worst of all, many of us were betrayed by our own countrymen. Rats who will get their just reward, damn them to hell.' Thierry spoke softly. 'Those of us who were left took refuge where we could, now that all our major links and lines of communication had been broken. I came to Marseille and found a tiny attic where I lived for a while to make sure I wasn't being watched before I was persuaded to come and live with maman. I took up my profession as chef again. Daily I thank God for my life and daily I pay tribute to all my dead friends. You must do the same. As should all of us.'

Claude was always curious to hear more of Thierry's great adventures, then unaware of their bearing on his own experiences. Thierry remained restrained, fearing the lad had known too much terror in his short life.

Thierry had reopened his own excellent restaurant in the suburbs of Marseille well known for its no-nonsense dishes. He had always cooked for the three of them on Saturdays; a Provence onion pie, pissaladière, or a bourride. Claude took no persuading to leave school at the first possible moment to start his training with Thierry. And there he stayed for several years, becoming sous-chef, appearing in the real world, making a living, whilst living inside in another world.

Then there was Jo's wedding.

Chapter 8

CLAUDE WOULD NOT REMEMBER HIS cousin Jo. He was a baby when Uncle Joseph, David's brother, and his wife, Mireille had left France for England with their child before the start of the war, disturbed by sinister changes since the advent of Adolph Hitler in 1933. They had been aware that many deaf ears were turned to news of events happening in Germany, that there were many who refused to believe the swell of anti-semitism unleashed and fuelled by the Nazi party. It had seemed to them astonishing that the persecution of Jews of medieval Europe or Tsarist Russia could be revived again in such a sophisticated, cultured part of Europe. Joseph had taken no chances, aware that history was constantly astonishing and did, indeed, repeat itself. He had tried vainly to encourage his brother, David, to take steps. They had both talked of German Jews they had lately met, heard the stories of their fearful flights from the rising tides of racism in their country. They knew that many German Jews had lost their jobs, were barred from schools, parks, theatres. There were stories of French Jews disappearing. Still David had refused to budge and told Joseph he was a coward to run away, not stand his ground. Joseph had been impatient with David and had wanted to shake him. He feared profoundly for the safety of his brother, Lily and the two children and deeply regretted they had parted acrimoniously.

Joseph had resigned from his job as history teacher at a lycée in Paris and taken his family to England to a close friend there who had welcomed them often for holidays, and had lately encouraged them to leave permanently, he, too, sensing menacing portents in Europe. Patrick was a fluent French speaker. He and Joseph had studied history together at the Sorbonne, becoming enduring friends. Joseph and Mireille responded to Patrick's insights and nudges and to his warmth. Distance from what was happening in Europe gave Patrick a wider political view of events than those peering more closely at the picture. Joseph trusted his friend's view and his own intuition. Mireille, too, felt a strong need to leave, especially now that they had a baby. The decision to go 'while they could' had upset David. It sowed seeds of doubt beneath his righteous determination to stay put. There had been a farewell dinner at Avenue Louis Blanc. David had often harked back to that evening. He would go over and over it with Lili.

'They left. My brother. Running away again. Always running. Telling us to do the same. Urging us! On and on about pogroms. I told them. We have to stop running sometime. You remember, Lili, I couldn't eat my chicken? Imagine, I couldn't eat my chicken! I told them they were cowards, d'you remember?' 'Stand up for your rights, Joseph. You're not a schmatte' I said. And Benjamin already gone.'

'Yes, I remember, David.' Her heart went out to her darling David, so anxious for the family, so full of conflicts and incipient doubts.

'And Joseph wanted my blessing. 'Come with us, come with us,' he said. D'you remember, Lili? I said: 'What, leave our beloved country? Why don't you stay here where you belong? Be courageous, face up to them for once, whoever they are. This is our home!' I said. 'Our children were born and brought up here. We don't want to live in England.' Didn't I say that Lily? And Joseph said, 'The least you can do is to give us your blessing'. You remember?'

'Yes, my love, that's what he said and we said we'd pray for them, d'you remember?' Lili knew why his eyes were shiny each time he scoured his memory. They had both been saddened that the parting had been full of anger between the two brothers. At chosen moments she had tentatively suggested that perhaps it would be expedient to leave. She had given up, unable to bear the reproachful look, heavy with 'not you, too, Lily.' She had loved David for his courage and ideals; so afraid, so brave; a romantic, sentimental and proud yet now tortured and torn. The reminiscences rummaged over the same words, redolent of fear and flux, of indecision. His words, raked over and over again, would begin to lose their potency. She thought perhaps she could persuade him to go down to Marseille to her mother's for a short while but doubted whether they'd be any better off there. Perhaps things would get better before long.

Joseph departed for England, events took their course and France became occupied, a possessed and impotent country reeling with humiliation and the fear that generates complicity. Lists of Jews in the préfecture grew; David could scarcely have ignored the tentacles reaching out from dark places to fasten onto their prey.

Patrick had found a flat for his friends, close to him in the suburbs of Manchester, a place called Cheetham Hill. Joseph's English was scant. He knew he would be unable to pursue his career as a teacher. Mireille had no English at all but was determined to learn and put down roots, given that they and their child were safe. Their little Jo would learn the language and absorb the culture naturally. They faced another culture, another life, the challenge of trying to belong somewhere else. They knew that they had had no choice but to leave France. David could not know the courage it had taken to uproot.

Joseph became apprenticed to a tailor, Daniel Freeman, found through a network of Jewish people, ready and eager to help refugees from Europe. He learned how to make patterns, to chalk on cloth, to measure, cut and sew. His teacher was a quiet patient man, a Jew who knew the problems of settling in a different country. His parents and his wife's parents had struggled and never really felt they belonged. Even he who had been brought up in England never lost a sense of dislocation. Joseph discovered the pleasure of making things for the first time in his life. He had labelled himself, without arrogance, 'intellectual' and had never before known the joy of absorption in crafting something elegant with his hands.

He learnt quickly, not only his new craft and his new language. Occasionally, as the two men bent over their work, Daniel would slide a brief remark over to his apprentice, a gift quietly offered to be taken home and put on display or hidden at the back of a drawer.

Joseph was growing to love and respect this taciturn man and knew that political and moral debates were 'hors de question.'

'Try not to be exclusive, Joseph. Make friends with Jews and Gentiles alike.'

His first gift. Joseph acknowledged that, apart from Patrick, his only contacts in this country were Jews and gave his first cadeau from Daniel to his wife. She accepted gracefully. She would not consign it to the back of the drawer.

Daniel watched his pupil with admiration and pride as he sliced through cloth.

'You're becoming very skilled, Joseph.'

'I have a good teacher.'

'You know, Joseph, Jews are never safe anywhere. We may think we are, like here, then we're not.' Joseph smiled as he continued his task and knew the wisdom of the words.

'Always try to fit in with the community. It's not your community remember. You are a guest. You may feel, as I do, that your soul is elsewhere.' Joseph was watching his teacher deftly sewing a shot silk lining into a navy blue waistcoat. He turned to his own task of pinning flimsy tissue paper patterns onto fine grey barathea.

'I hope my son Jo will feel at home here as perhaps I never will. He's very young.'

Daniel, with masterly hands, completed his beautiful artefact without another word.

Jo did not disappoint his father. Like blotting paper he absorbed the language and the culture of North Manchester and unwittingly showed his parents the way. Being 'accepted' was not a conscious endeavour for him. He knew of his Uncle David and the family in

Paris but there had been no contact between them since the bitter farewell dinner together. Joseph had sent letters in the early days after their departure but received no word and soon understood from Patrick that his attempts to communicate may endanger his brother and Lili and the children. He understood, too, what it meant to have a heavy heart. The silence and uncertainty about his family were a constant cause of anxiety.

Even so, Joseph and Mireille began to embrace their new life, Mireille picking up the language quickly, working in a bakery near to their home. She worked hard at learning the language knowing how key that was to being accepted, fitting in. Jo integrated easily and did well at school. The occupation of their country filled them with fear. They all heard eventually of the fate of David and Lili and Rose and the miraculous escape of Claude. Joseph never recovered from the shock and prayed every day for forgiveness. He knew his brother had been naive and had, in that context, a misplaced sense of pride in his family and his family's French nationality. Joseph had known what his probable fate would be if he had stayed put and now knew that he hadn't tried hard enough to persuade David to leave. He said many times to Mireille, 'If only we had insisted more we could have persuaded him. Instead we had an angry row on our last night together. God forgive me.' Mireille argued that it was David and Lili's choice and nothing they could have said would have changed their minds. She was no less devastated by the horror of their deaths but felt no sense of guilt except for the guilt that most survivors felt for simply being alive. They had a photograph in a silver frame in the centre of the sideboard, David and Lili standing behind the two children with their hands on their shoulders, looking happy and hopeful.

Joseph decided he would write regularly to Claude to give him news of the 'English family' and to invite him to visit them. He was disappointed to receive scant news in return and no mention of the invitation. Joseph thought that probably Claude would not wish to be reminded of his lost family by his uncle whom he had known well up to their departure and may even be ashamed of him leaving them and fleeing to another country. He would have to try and live with that thought which echoed his brother's sentiments.

Joseph and Mireille didn't mind that their son, Jo, was marrying a Gentile. It was the time to be less exclusive. This opinion did not altogether meet with approval from some of their Jewish friends who were respectful enough of the right of choice to confine their objections to quips. 'Who'll cook the bacon and sausages for breakfast?' 'You read it in The Merchant of Venice—in converting Jews to Christians you raise the price of pork!' 'You know what they say, Jo? When you baptise a Jew hold him under the water for five minutes.' If Jane's parents minded their daughter marrying a Jew they didn't show it. They adored Jo. He was close to his parents and even as a young boy, becoming thoroughly Mancunian, he could see they had problems in those early days, adapting to a new life and speaking a new language. Now, about to leave the family home to live with Jane, he felt quite at ease, seeing them enjoying their lives and friends. He was proud of what they had done, leaving their home in Paris and courageously building a new life. He found his father's occasional slides into melancholy, guilt, remorse difficult to understand even when his mother, Mireille, tried to explain that these sentiments were all too common amongst survivors of the Holocaust. He asked her why she never seemed to experience these feelings. She had replied, 'The reason for that is standing right in front of me asking me these questions.'

A civil wedding was planned and a sumptuous reception, kosher, at Joseph and Mireille's house. Their dining room was large, panelled in oak, furnished with a dark heavy dining table with bulbous legs and chairs to match, pictures, mostly victorian, silk lined curtains in dark red, and candelabra attached to the panelling. It was stifling but a suitable place for an 'occasion' and for the formal Friday night suppers.

Claude Blum, much to the surprise of the family, had accepted to be guest of honour. It had been Jo's idea to ask him. He wanted his parents to connect again with their Parisian family, especially his father whose anguish over leaving his brother, Lily, Rose and

Claude sometimes spilled out. And Claude may enjoy being with his family. Jo hoped that he and Claude may become good friends. Claude had struggled to reply to his uncle's letters, feeling he no longer knew them, that they were in a different world, but he had been greatly encouraged by Thierry to stay in touch with them. He always received warm letters and when the invitation came to be guest of honour he was at once touched and terrified, resistant to the idea. Spurred on by Thierry he decided to accept and at last see his family in Cheetham Hill. Thierry, keen for him to break out of the shell he was in, set about, from the day the invitation arrived, persuading him that he should go; it was his duty, he owed it to his parents and Rose to celebrate a happy event, it would be impolite to refuse. Claude gave in to Thierry somehow unable to stand up to him. 'Chez Tamille' sounded like a fairy-tale place. He had learned that the family had a great bond with the family of Daniel, Joseph's boss and it was agreed that Sarah, Daniel's granddaughter, would meet him at Heathrow Airport and take him by car to the North of England. Sarah had studied French at university and, apart from her, only Joseph and Mireille spoke French, Jo a little, hearing his parents often conversing in their native tongue. Sarah offered to meet Claude since everyone else seemed occupied with the preparations. And she was curious.

What had not been decided was how the two would recognise each other. Two weeks before Claude's arrival a supper had been arranged by Joseph and Mireille, an intimate affair with close family and friends, to put some final touches to the wedding day arrangements including deciding how Sarah and Claude would know each other at Heathrow the day before the event. There had been talk of a pink carnation, a rendez-vous at the French Airways desk. All very sensible. As the wine flowed the suggestions became more colourful. Maybe Sarah should dress as a nun, easily spotted in a crowd. Claude could wear a yamulka spiked with daffodils. Sarah might wave a wand topped with a spangled Star of David. Imagine Claude encased in a sandwich board with 'sholom aleichem' in large letters. The happy family joked and anticipated the joy of embracing Claude whose life they all knew had cost dearly.

Sarah had heard about Claude's history and wondered how he might feel being taken care of by his grandmother and uncle. Though she loved her grandparents immensely she had experienced many frustrations. She never answered them back, because they were elderly and one didn't treat elderly people like that. And it was only in that period before she left that Josie let fly at them. They were both always polite, always willing to give a helping hand. And however rebellious they felt they kept it to themselves. They had felt obligated to their grandparents for taking them in. And the couple were so 'out of date', just not 'in touch'. Sarah knew it wasn't a 'normal' upbringing and wondered if this Claude had felt the same things. Perhaps his uncle had been more like a dad than ever Daniel could have been.

At the same moment Claude was nervously sharing supper with his uncle Thierry who had refused his invitation, unable to spare the time to go to England due to business pressures. Thierry had no wish to go. He still felt bitter that his brother-in-law, Joseph, had taken the family to England, deserting the cause, even though they were still alive as a result; that they hadn't all moved to a safer place in France. He of all people knew that there weren't any safe places and that he was being irrational. Except even survivors never really escape.

Claude's head seethed with anxieties. He had only a few words and phrases in English learned specially for the foreign clientele in the restaurant. And what should he wear? He had no formal clothes. Would the men be dressed in the strange suits and hats he had seen in wedding photographs in magazines? What would he take for a wedding present? Who would meet him? How would he know who they were? And would they speak French? Thierry calmed the usually quiet, reflective young man and tried to reassure him. He wisely advised Claude to wear what he would wear at a French wedding. They would buy him a light grey suit, a white silk shirt and a silver grey tie. Thierry offered to lend him his diamond tie-stud. They decided against a dashing cummerbund in deference to English reserve. They bought expensive soft black leather lace-up shoes which Claude would wear an hour a day to break them in. And what else to take to wear?

'You know,' Thierry explained, 'the English are either terribly well dressed, for occasions, or otherwise very badly dressed. They don't have the chic that we French have.'

'So I'd better go to the flea market for the rest of my stuff!'

'No, jeune homme, you need to show them how we dress smartly yet casually. It's called style. Two pairs of dark grey pure wool trousers—it'll be September and bloody freezing in England.'

Claude wondered, how his uncle came to be such an authority on all things English. He was a little bit sceptical. Thierry continued.

'A navy blue cashmere jacket, white shirts and a couple of discreet Hermes ties. And a dark mackintosh. It never stops raining over there. That should do it. As for the wedding present, something typically French; tasteful in other words. And something you can carry on the aeroplane. Yes, I know. A silver plateau for hors d'oeuvres. Now, what else? Don't worry about the language. You'll have Joseph and Mireille and I expect Jo will know a bit.'

Claude was ready to back out. That was why Thierry had been so 'knowledgeable' and uncharacteristically assertive. He was determined Claude would make this trip. He worried about his state of mind and hoped that the stimulation of the trip would draw him out of his deep reserve.

Daniel had the bright idea that they should exchange photographs. Sarah had only ever seen one photo from Marseille, a black and white snap. Joseph and Mireille had been so proud of it. The elderly lady, Alice, in black from top to toe, silver haired, birdlike yet radiating strength and dignity, was standing straight as a ramrod looking disapprovingly at the photographer and clearly not enjoying the attention. Next to her was Thierry, her son, tall, gaunt, in dark trousers and a pin-striped waistcoat, a watch chain suspended from one of its buttons, trailing into his trouser pocket, dressily contrasting with his thick white collarless shirt undone at the neck. He had a surprising shock of blond hair and pale searching eyes. And there was Claude at his side, a young lad in grey knee-length trousers held up by braces, a short sleeved open necked shirt, stick like arms and legs, his black smoothed down hair rebelling against the slickness. He looked mistrustful. Unsmiling, the three stood to attention in a line, on the cobbles in front of their terraced house.

Joseph and Mireille had told Sarah of Claude's past; at least, as much as they knew: his escape, the fate of his family, his new life and career in Marseille. She waited impatiently for a recent photograph to arrive to match it to the old one and his story. She felt strangely drawn to him, to his history, the loss of his family and wondered how he dealt with such tragedy. In the photo of him as a child he seemed wary, uncertain and apart. They looked like hard-working folk in a rather shabby environment, a street and house not too unlike that of her grandparents when she was a child, but with shutters. She knew the two French families kept in touch and wondered if she had been mentioned in the letters from Joseph and his family and if this man was aware of her own family and their hardships and tragedies. It intrigued her why she was giving him so much thought. He would probably come over and perform his duties as 'guest of honour' and then return to Marseille, family duty done. It was hard to imagine this aloof child in the photograph amongst his loving family in their apartment in Paris and even harder to think of the events that had overtaken him. 'God knows how such experiences may have shaped him,' she had thought. 'I wonder what he looks like now. Well I shall soon find out.'

Claude had kept up a scant correspondence with his family in the north of England. He was not fond of writing, pushed into it by his uncle, and anyway he had little to say to these people he had never met. Now he unearthed several photographs he had received over the years. He was familiar with pictures of his family in England but they meant nothing. Uncle Joseph was always smiling and seemed to be increasingly overweight in contrast to the slim serious looking tante Mireille. The more he looked at Joseph's picture the more he realised how like his own father he was. Jo resembled his father astonishingly. There was only one photograph of Sarah, aged about fifteen, amongst a group of family and friends. She and her sister Josie were standing between their grandparents, behind Joseph, Mireille, Jo and two people he didn't know at all sitting cross-legged on the grass. It was a 'snap' taken in Joseph's garden, rather fuzzy but clear enough to see happy people in summery clothes with their arms round each other. Sarah's grandmother, who he remembered was called Sophie, looked pointed and angular, rather fearsome even though smiling. Daniel, the grandfather, was a silvery man, dignified, a philosopher. Claude could scarcely make out Josie. She had moved at the crucial moment, a dark blur. He had hardly given this photograph a second glance before. Most of what he could see of Sarah was a mop of thick black curly hair and a wide smile. He peered at her intently hoping to find more. Simply gazing at her the others around melted into grey. He continued to gaze. She was looking at him now. He liked her. She liked him. They were linked he was sure. A strange feeling that he knew her suffused him. A little afraid of his inexplicable sense of intimacy he drew back from the image to include the other faces again and break the spell. It was time for work, time to become absorbed in an evening's cooking, to indulge his clients.

A short formal note expressing good wishes was paper-clipped to the photograph for Sarah from Marseille, Thierry and Claude standing in front of their unpretentious little restaurant, Thierry holding a piece of paper up in the air. It seems the restaurant had won a coveted prize in spite of its rather dowdy façade. The aprons and chef's hats gleamed their whiteness against dull red brick walls. Thierry beamed with pleasure and pride, the thin face crinkling, his tall body stiffly straight. Claude, shorter though tall and slight, looked lugubrious and aloof, appearing shy of expressing joy. Sarah thought him 'interesting' but not handsome. She saw a lot of darkness in his face, a shadowy chin, a rather pouting mouth and most striking, his large hostile eyes. Perhaps he was posing, a doleful Herbert Lom, a smouldering Lawrence Olivier. Thierry beside him, vivaciously good looking in a thin angular way, brimming with vitality, contrasted sharply with his nephew, his young apprentice. The new photograph was an echo of the earlier one of the much younger Claude. His wary eyes looked too big for his face, his body evidently thin behind the apron, his chef's toque straight as a turret; no jauntiness about this young man. Sarah stared at the face, attracted yet strangely disquieted.

He was nothing like his uncle Joseph. Well, Joseph did have a dark swarthiness about him and large full lips, but he was round, no sharp edges, a man who enjoyed life to the full, a bon viveur. He too had been spared the death camps and had told Sarah he thanked God every day. Sarah would, without doubt, recognise this sombre young man at the airport and tried to substitute the chef's uniform and dress him in casual clothes, a leather jacket topped off with a dark well cut head of hair. She felt singularly excited.

Claude was taken aback when he drew the photograph out of its envelope. He ignored for a long time the note which had been enclosed. It was a studio portrait in colour against a pale, undistracting background, of a young woman smiling, on the verge of laughter; a mass of black wiry hair, long, well cut yet unruly; an immediate impression of gaiety and beauty. He was captivated. He loved the wideness of her cheekbones, the large smile showing even, neat white teeth. She brimmed with energy. But above all, he saw compassion and felt again an inexplicable bond with her. She looked straight at him bringing a smile and a lightness.

Now the old letters were re-read with minute attention instead of the cursory scan they had had on receipt. He felt sure she had been mentioned several times and set about finding every reference he could to her and her family. The grandparents, Sophie and Daniel, had taken care of her and her sister after the house in Manchester and their mother had been bombed. Claude had paid little attention to the letters they had received in the past. Their plights had nothing to do with his life. The careful reading of letters he had only scanned as a youngster jolted him out of his self-possessed torment for a moment. This girl, Sarah, whose photograph he stared at, had in faraway England, been stricken by different means at the hands of those who had taken his own family away.

It seemed Sophie and Daniel had looked after the Blum family so well, uncle Joseph apprenticed to Daniel, the two families becoming intertwined and supportive, mindful of their mutual struggles. Not a mention of Sarah's father. Josie had left Cheetham Hill and, praise be, Sarah had a degree in modern languages and had returned to

Cheetham Hill. There was no more he could glean. He suddenly remembered the note which had been sent with the photograph and, seizing upon it, read of good wishes for him and his uncle and an impatience to meet him, all expressed in impeccable French. He found himself longing to meet her and to know all about her. Looking at her face he wanted to tell, for the first time ever, of his childhood, the details he had withheld, the despair, fear, loneliness, things seen and heard, all imprisoned inside him. Looking at her face again he smiled back and told her he loved her. He did not remember ever feeling so animated and said aloud, 'I do not need to feel guilty.' He hadn't known until now, seeing the photograph, the gazing, that it was guilt that consumed him. Sarah's image brought back words of his grandmother, words climbing out of the depths of his memory, retrieved inexplicably by a photograph, words which otherwise would have been unheard.

'Claude, ma puce, you will never forget, and I don't know how these memories will leave you. I hope you will be happy. But you will be left with guilt.' At the time Claude listened to his grandmother, Alice, and stored her words without comprehending.

'You are not responsible, mon chou. Tu n'es pas coupable. You are blameless. Always remember that.' Her words, several years on, now filled his ears. 'You are blameless.' It wasn't due to him that his family had perished. He was not responsible. He had been spared and he was not to blame for the fate of his beloved family. 'I will keep them around me forever, Mamie. Maman, papa, Rose will stay with me I promise. We'll be together again, you'll see.'

Suddenly he felt afraid that he had invested so heavily in a photograph. He returned it to its envelope, embarrassed by his soaring fantasies. Sarah would probably have a lover. And would probably find him unattractive and dull. After all, she was only meeting him because the others were so busy with the wedding. And she could speak French.

A surge of people flooded the concourse at Heathrow where Sarah waited, the long delay shredding her excitement into neurotic thoughts.

'He won't be a bundle of laughs that's for sure from his photo. He'll be gagged with shyness. Hell, those stretches of motorway ahead, confined in a metal box, in silence. We'll take an instant dislike to each other. Shall I kiss him or shake hands? He's sure to have a strong Marseillais accent and I won't understand him. I wish I'd never agreed to this. God, I've forgotten already where I've parked the car. Will it be 'tu' or 'vous?"

Her eyes scanned the teeming arrivals and found him within seconds. He spotted her at the same moment. They waved tentatively and made their way toward each other. Before they came face to face they each had time to observe the other. Sarah saw a tall, graceful man walking towards her, not handsome but not unattractive, wearing a smart dark jacket, white shirt, discreet blue tie with red spots, carrying an expensive looking leather holdall. He was smiling, an expression she could scarcely have imagined from the gloomy photos of him. Claude walked towards the barrier where Sarah was waiting and saw a tall, dark curly-haired young woman with a big smile. She looked smart he thought, in jeans and a red silk shirt. She was even more beautiful than in her photo. Claude put down his bag and without hesitation, assured and elegant, he kissed her on both cheeks. Sarah was bowled over. She was the one to be stunned into silence. Claude had shed his nervousness the second he saw her. He was greeting someone he knew.

'Bonjour, Sarah. Je suis très content de te rencontrer.' A deep voice with only a slight accent and already calling her 'tu'.

'Bonjour, Claude. Moi aussi. C'est un grand plaisir.' The reality exposed the limitations of a photograph being but a split second's glimpse of a life. Most people want to look their best in that moment. Sarah had been pleased with the photograph she had sent. Claude was not happy with his but it had been the only one he could find. The photographs had deceived, as they do.

Claude had not seen the sadness behind the vivacious smile, a sadness which enhanced her beauty. Sarah had not seen the quiet eloquence and assuredness behind the doleful, gangly image she had carried in her head. There was no sense of gloom or aloofness about him. She would only later discover the accuracy of her first impressions.

'Thank you for coming to meet me.' He spoke rather slowly, deeply and smiled straight into Sarah's eyes, almost too intimately, Sarah had thought. She returned his smile.

'A pleasure.' And wondered why she felt more nervous than earlier. She silently asked herself, 'Why the hell am I feeling like a teenager on my first date? Come on, Sarah, get a grip. You're a mature, experienced, street-wise woman, twenty eight years old, don't be so bloody silly.'

Claude picked up his bag, took hold of her hand and asked, 'So which way?' Sarah prayed to a god she didn't believe in to enlist help to find the car. And it seemed her prayer was answered.

By the time they arrived at Cheetham Hill they had talked easily, laughed a little, compared bits of their lives, delicately exchanging stories, glancing at each other swiftly and often. Sarah told of the closeness of the two families and the special bond between Joseph and her grandfather. She explained briskly the events which had led to living with her grandparents, the difficulties they had experienced coming to terms with their mother's death, Josie's waywardness and eventual departure. She was surprised at her frankness about parts of her life she tended to keep locked inside her. Claude sensitively encouraged her. He, for his part, talked of his work as a chef, the loss of his grandmother, Thierry's bravery; and no mention of his life in Paris and how he had ended up in Marseille.

The young man was welcomed by his family with a warmth and gaiety which brought back to him the atmosphere of his childhood home. Joseph, so like David, vividly restored the image of his father and called back, even more potently, the face of his mother. Joseph even sounded like papa.

Benjamin and his wife, Esther, had arrived earlier from New York. Claude could not recognise this frail elderly man. The Benjamin he knew from his childhood was chubby, garrulous and full of vitality. He would not spend much time with this old man who was not Benjamin to him.

To his surprise Claude enjoyed the wedding and found he could speak more English than he thought; the polite, social kind he had acquired for their English clientele. He was drawn to his family and especially to Joseph whose presence drew him more intensely to his world in Paris. Now he was sure he knew why Sarah seemed familiar to him, why he had loved her from the photographs. She was Rose. There were things about her which evoked Rose so vividly, her dark curly hair, her vivacity and energy. Sarah would become Rose. Of course, Rose was now the same age. He had every reason to want to stay in this milieu. He could transform the visual and auditory resemblances into reality. He set his sights on marrying Sarah to keep Rose with him and they'd live close to Joseph to enjoy the presence of his father. He was certain it had all been meant and could never have seen any reason to feel the slightest remorse for his undisclosed motives. His existence on the edge was to be endured. Everything was there to serve his ruthless dedication to a life with his parents and his sister.

He felt a huge sense of freedom. He experienced happiness for the first time since his childhood and excitement at the prospect of being with his parents and Rose again. Thierry would not have recognised this animated young man. Claude knew that he would have to play a role with these people on the surface of his inner world. He felt well practised after his performance as Jean-Pierre Bonnard. The Fathers had condoned the deceit and lying that was necessary so his conscience was undisturbed by a thought that what he was embarking on may be immoral and exploitative. He would be with his family in Paris and he would take any steps to achieve his goal.

Sarah was captivated by this mysterious young man and flattered when he told her he had decided to stay on longer than he'd planned because he wanted to be with her. She was delighted, excited and in love. The families, with the exception of Sophie, nodded their approval at what had become a whirlwind love affair. Sarah now knew at first hand the meaning of being 'swept off one's feet'. It had never happened before, the lightheadedness, the utter absorption in another person and in oneself. Her unspoken question was, 'I wonder how long this lasts?' He had wanted to see the countryside around Manchester and Sarah decided the Peak District and Buxton would be the place. Claude said he would make all the arrangements and Sarah wondered about the sleeping arrangements in particular. It was clear they were in love but so far had only kissed. Sarah rather liked Claude's reticence and thought he was waiting for them to be away from the families. When they arrived she found he had booked two single rooms in their individual names. Having a drink in the bar after they'd put their stuff in their own rooms, Sarah, astonishing herself by her temerity, said, 'You're a virgin, aren't you?'

'Yes,' he said looking straight at her. She was impressed by his frankness, expecting indignation.

'Would you like to change that?'

'Yes,' he said. Perhaps he was suppressing his fears, excitement.

'Well let's change the booking to a double room.'

'That's a bit embarrassing. They'll think I'm . . . .'

'Who cares what they think?'

She thought it a bit odd that this young Frenchman had never had a relationship but, well, what did she know? Her own history wasn't exactly full of moonlight and roses.

He was shyly inexperienced in bed but Sarah was confident that, given time, 'things would change.'

Sophie thought the young man was 'not what he seemed'.

'He's only been here five minutes and he's got his feet under at least two tables. And he can hardly speak English. No good'll come of this, you'll see.' Such misgivings were expressed to anyone who would listen to the chunterings of an increasingly frail old lady. No-one shared her view.

Claude returned to Marseille to tell his uncle of his intentions to marry and settle in England. Thierry was delighted—it would be a fresh start, new beginnings. The kid had dwelt too much in the past since he had, just that once, acknowledged the fate of his family. It had never been mentioned again. Thierry had watched his nephew retreat, from that moment, into long, wistful silences increasingly disturbing to those who knew him. He always worked well and had become a good chef under Thierry's tutelage. Yet the young man was more and more aloof. Thierry had begun to fear for him. He had overheard him talking to himself in his bedroom, a place where he took refuge as often as was civilly acceptable. It was as if he had become programmed. Even his speech had become mechanical; polite greetings, questions and comments. His behaviour was predictable right up to the last 'Good night, tonton. Sleep well.' Except for the time he spent in his room. Thierry worried about the low murmurings he could hear but knew intuitively not to ask. When Claude returned from England the change in him was astonishing. He still spent time in his own room, and the murmurings continued but there was a lightness, even gaiety about him which Thierry had never seen. The news of his feelings for Sarah was entirely welcome even if it meant Thierry would be on his own. That was alright; he was tired, needed solitude. He still endured sleepless nights and symptoms of shock every time there was a knock on the door. The sound of the voice of a German tourist in the restaurant took his breath away and filled his vision momentarily with grey uniforms in the streets and squares of Bordeaux. A car backfiring would cause him to tense up and begin to crouch. But more than the physical aftermath, he was left with the bitter taste of mistrust, disillusion and fear. His life had lost its sense of wonder and curiosity. Worst of all he had lost his respect for the dignity of human life. Perhaps his young nephew would triumph over the effects of his experiences now that he had the chance of a new life in a new country. Thierry would decline his invitation to the wedding on the grounds that he couldn't leave the Café D'Or for so long. In truth he felt he would be out of his depth in Claude's new life and would provide unwelcome reminders. And he wasn't sure how he would be with Joseph and Mireille. He would be better left to himself

Chapter 9

THE WEDDING WAS A SIMPLE, civic ceremony followed by yet another lavish reception full of joy, dancing and kletzmer. Two weddings in the family, two happy couples and the prospect of children free from the traumatic aftermath of the war; a fresh beginning, new lives, prosperity and relief. Joseph's hour-long toast said as much, in as many ways as he could think of, accompanied by tears and cheers, more champagne and still more kletzmer sentiment.

Sarah knew for the first time what it meant to 'be in love' and had had no hesitation accepting Claude's proposal of marriage. She surprised herself being usually rather cautious by nature. Equally surprising was how carefree she felt, full of the sense that she could do anything, and resented every moment she was not with Claude. The couple saw to it that there were very few of those.

Claude had charm, attractively halting English and Gallic smoothness to captivate all but one of his new family. Sophie, forever wary, particularly of foreigners, not that she knew many and somehow making no link to her own antecedents, looked him up and down when they met at the reception as he focussed his winning ways on her, taking account of her pale fragile thinness and bearing in mind her reputation as a tough disputatious force.

'I am enchanted to meet you again.'

'Really? We say 'pleased', 'pleased to meet you.' You should know that. I suppose you prefer French cooking to our less fussy ways?'

'Not at all, Madame. It's hard to say,' Claude replied, as tactfully as he could.

'I see. I myself tend to be decisive.'

'I am sure you are,' Claude replied with a light, over polite smile and formal little nod.

Daniel stood by, amused.

Sophie spoke slowly, deliberately, her way of mocking his loose grasp of the language.

'Do you intend to stay in England?'

'Of course, Madame. I don't take Sarah away from home.'

Sophie let the misuse of tense go.

'And what about your home?'

'I am at home here.'

'That was quick! And decisive. I hope you are serious, young man. All we want is for Sarah to be happy.' Sophie pierced him with her eyes.

'Moi aussi. Me also.'

"Me too' we say. What a good job she speaks French!'

'I learn quick.'

'Quickly,' she corrected again.

'Yes, quickly. Thank you. You are very helpful, Madame.'

'We will all need to be.'

Sophie, bristling, turned to talk to Joseph about his extravagant reception, determined she would dislike this young man. Barely out of earshot she said, 'No-one's ever that nice and charming when they've been through what he's been through. It's a veneer covering up God knows what. He's not what he seems, that's all I can say.' Joseph was the butt of her compounding irritation but he knew her ways and loved them. And what's more she was so often spot on. In any case it was as clear as daylight that Claude and Sarah would make a very happy couple. And Joseph had found a way to diminish his guilt a little. He would do all he could to help his nephew. He had started well, providing the lavish wedding breakfast and booking a good hotel in London for the start of their honeymoon. He would help them buy a house nearby. They'd go short of nothing. Joseph reflected every day on his good fortune. He had had a wonderful teacher in Daniel whose business he took over when Daniel retired. He remembered with a smile that, at the time of the signing over of the business, Sophie had said to Daniel, well within earshot, 'From rags to riches and back again, you mark my words.' Happily, and so far, she had been wrong. The business had gone from strength to strength to three men's outfitters in the neighbourhood, two of them in the increasingly affluent parts, Prestwich and Heaton Park. And now he had the chance to take away some of the pain from the thorn in his side. Claude's arrival was a blessing.

But not for Sophie.

'He's strange,' she said to Daniel as they shared a pot of tea in their kitchen. 'There's something about him. It makes me uneasy.'

'He seems like a nice young man to me,' Daniel offered, gently. 'Given the terrible experiences he's had he's ready to move forward into a new life. He was very happy in our company and they obviously love each other. I can't remember our Sarah looking so happy.'

'That's what worries me. I know in my bones, Daniel, that he's trouble. I can't quite explain it.' She refilled the tea cups, searching for the words. 'It's like he's playing a part, being charming, wanting to win us over. In a way, seducing everyone, not least, our Sarah.'

'Well of course he wants endear himself to the families and it's difficult for him when his English isn't quite fluent.'

'Not quite fluent?' Sophie said, sarcastically. 'I've heard two year olds talk better! No, Daniel, it's more than that.'

'He *is* a stranger in a foreign country trying to get to grips with it all and the families he hardly knows yet. Give him credit.'

'I know that. I'm just worried for Sarah.'

'If they love each other that's all that matters, isn't it?'

Sophie got up to rinse the cups in the sink.

'We'll see.'

'Maiden, my maiden. It could be the making of Sarah. As far as we know she's never been courting in a serious way. Look at how radiant she is. Let's be happy for her.'

'I wish I had your confidence, Daniel. For me, it's just like watching someone, an actor, playing a part on the stage. There's no—how can I put it—no sincerity. That's the word. I hope I'm wrong.'

'Me also, my love!'

Claude had no difficulty finding work as a chef in the restaurant of a good class hotel in Manchester. It was not he who described the restaurant as 'good class.' That was its reputation, quite unmerited in Claude's view. In any case, for him, it was a job he could do well and easily with no great demands on his English or his inner world. Sarah continued teaching and they could afford to buy a modest house, with some help from Joseph, close to their families. It was a rather sombre Edwardian terraced house which hadn't been decorated or cared for in any way for many years. Sarah could see how it might be transformed and felt excited by plans to paint, make curtains, create a garden full of pots of flowers and climbing plants to cover the dull brick walls of the back yard. Spring and summer bulbs would do well in the little front garden. Their bedroom would be white and pale blue, and the little box room next door could be made into a fresh and pretty bathroom. They would knock down the wall which separated the tiny kitchen from the dining room, then there'd be so much more light. Claude would love the paintings and re-upholstered chairs in the sitting room; he would spend a lot of time there apart after the late hours at the restaurant and in the early hours when he planned his menus. Lots of creamy-white paint and a sewing machine would make all the difference. Of course, there was never enough time to discuss the details as Claude worked most evenings meaning they spent precious little time together. Sarah accepted that, due to the nature of Claude's work, that was how it had to be whether she liked it or not. And she didn't, troubled that they seemed not to be sharing as she would have liked.

It has started so well but Sarah experienced a distance she couldn't explain and which Claude claimed didn't exist. She had been swept off her feet and loved the feeling. She knew they had a long way to go before they would know each other really well but was soon disappointed by Claude's reluctance to talk about his life before he arrived in Marseille. She would be patient knowing what a devastating period it had been, and felt sure that, given time, he would be able to share his experiences. As the months went by he was no nearer to opening up and that sense of distance seemed to be growing for Sarah. She began to worry about their marriage.

Sarah went ahead with transforming the house. 'Go ahead, my love. Vas-y. Do what you think is best. You know I have not much time to think about these things. Please do what you would like. I want you to be a happy girl.' Claude often called Sarah 'girl'. She was left with a free hand to make the home 'their own', and a lead weight of disappointment; two ways. She confided later to a friend, Harriet: 'He was not interested in the slightest in our home together. And what's more, after a very short time, he lost interest in me and in making love.' Harriet was the only person she could ever have told.

'I know that happens with couples after years but we'd been married less than a year. I always made the first move and sometimes he responded but more often than not he'd pat me and tell me how tired he was and how he needed to be up so early in the mornings. He spends hours in that sitting room, all to do with getting home late, needing a cognac and time to plan his buying and his menus. Ships passing in the night. He's so distant. OK, he's always polite, affectionate, but—he's just not interested in, well, me.' The promise of a happy marriage had faded so quickly. Claude was kind, polite, never argumentative yet still, in some strange way, detached, not quite wholehearted in what they did together, even when making love. In exasperation she would sometimes confront him with her disappointment. He never raised his voice, always told her he loved her and would do so for ever and that it was his nature to be a bit withdrawn. Perhaps, Sarah thought, having an affectionate and faithful partner was a lot to be thankful for.

After two years Sarah became pregnant, a small miracle Sarah thought given the rarity of their love-making. Weeks passed before she told Claude, anticipating she didn't know what except that it wouldn't be sheer delight. She finally told him when they lunched together on his off-day. He spoke several appropriate words on being told, with mismatched intonation, dynamics and body language. 'Oh, Sarah, I can hardly believe it,' with a falling cadence. 'You have taken my breath. You, and a baby in your arms it's . . .' His facial expression verged on repulsion. 'It's fine and you must take care of yourself and rest a lot . . . .' He embraced her with the warmth of a shadow and removed himself from the table to make his way to his little sitting room in a welter of fear and turmoil that such an intrusion and complication was about to be introduced into his world.

'I don't want a baby,' he hissed as he walked into his sitting room. 'She was supposed to be on the pill. How dare she be pregnant! I don't need a baby. I just don't need that in my life. It's the last thing I want!' He banged the table with his fist, sat down and retreated into thoughts of other things.

He was kind and helpful during the pregnancy but refused to be present at the birth. And he did all the right and proper things but with no heart in any of it, speaking appropriate words but without depth. From the beginning he had seemed sometimes aloof, a bit odd, not always quite present, like someone taking on a different persona. Sarah felt afraid of knowing what the problem might be. She was shocked by the lack of feeling and interest he showed towards their daughter, right from the start. Sarah had thought that, once he saw the baby, their child, he would be thrilled and proud. It was utterly incomprehensible to her and filled her with anxiety about her future in this marriage, about the effect of his indifference on their daughter, about her loss of passion for this man. It had all changed so quickly after such an auspicious beginning. 'How will I be able to stay in this situation?' she wondered. The question was never far from her mind and the constant ringing of 'Why? Why is he like this?' It was bewildering to her and painfully stressful. And humiliating.

On Naomi's fourth birthday she faced the fact that Claude was a long way from normal. Her misgivings had grown. She was fully aware of the traumatic experiences in his life and the terrible losses. She had made allowances for the effects of such tragedy. But time had passed now and it was time to move on.

It was one very early morning when she couldn't sleep, about two a.m. when she heard the sounds. Claude had not yet come to bed. She crept downstairs, trembling, anticipating something frightening, and, listening outside the little sitting room, heard talking, a voice, Claude's, but talking like a child to his mother telling her he'd finished his homework and how easy it was. Then a silence. And then a reply as if he'd been spoken to. 'Yes, of course I will. I'll go and tell papa and help him close up the shop.' She had sometimes heard him mumbling a bit and hadn't thought it anything to worry too much about. But not like this. 'Supper's ready, papa . . . . I'm not telling you. It's a surprise.' She ran back upstairs unsure if this was real or a nightmare she was having. She was cold through to her bone marrow and feigned sleep when he came to bed, her head trying to make sense of what she had heard and not succeeding. She crept down again the following night and several more nights after and listened in horror to more of

Claude's childlike voice talking to his family. 'I'll help you with your maths, Rose. I'm good at maths, aren't I, maman? Be quick, though. Uncle Benjamin's coming tonight and we'll have our concert.' It was the most chilling experience she had ever had and a kind of mad despair overtook her. Her emotions began to tumble one after the other, into her head and body, sometimes simultaneously, out of control; anger, bewilderment, regret, calm, self-pity, pity for Claude, profound sadness, fear. She felt brittle as if she could break into pieces at any time. She had to try to appear to be normal going about her daily life and knew that the days of trying to confront Claude with her fears and her questions were over. He simply was neither listening or caring. There was no point. Someone else would have to tackle him. In her attempts to try to conduct herself in an outwardly normal fashion everything began to feel drab and dull, even the brightness she had created in their home, the sound of Mozart, the taste of fresh raspberries, conversations, grass, sky. Her perceptions altered so much it was as if she were living in slow motion. Sounds took their time to arrive in her ears, a running person ran impossibly slowly. And why were people talking so slowly? The channels into her senses were closing up like the changed world of a drug addict.

She wanted to punish him, hurt him. How dare he opt for a life apart from her? What kind of crazy life is he living? He was distorting her mind. An unfamiliar and irresistible force to destroy him took her over, a powerful urge to be separate from him, to remove him from her life and the lives of her family and especially her daughter. He was unreal, a terrible spectre. How could she possibly tell her family of the monster they harboured amongst them, of her growing sense of feeling mad, out of touch?

The talk went on and on inside her head. 'What the hell am I going to do? Live a lie? Pretend all is well when all is far from being well? Plenty of people do, ashamed to show the world that they haven't got things right in their lives. Muffled by pride. Keep up appearances for the sake of what people will think. Is that how my life will be? God in heaven, you don't exist. Or if you do give me a hand! Do nothing, do nothing for the time being. Carry on, work, be with the folks. Say nothing, say nothing for the time being. Is that an opt-out? I don't know but that's my instinct right now. What would I like at this moment?' A question she often posed. The response was always the same. 'To love and be loved.'

Naomi was her bright light, the one who would bring her back to her senses, a child who was embraced and rather spoilt by all the family, a little precocious, and appearing not to mind too much that she scarcely saw her father. Claude's aloofness, couched in polite responses, never wavered. The demands of her child and her teaching brought Sarah slowly back to normal pace and a place of acceptance and growing understanding that her husband was mentally very ill, traumatised by his childhood experiences, and couldn't help the way he was. For the time being she would play her part. And she would try to get help for him. For the sake of the child, the family and Claude, the pretence of normality to the outside world became her modus vivendi. First she had to set about persuading Claude that he needed help. Sarah wasn't hopeful but had a strong intuitive feeling that, at the moment, she needed to stay in this house, look after her daughter and be with her sick husband.

The family spoke amongst themselves of Claude's aloofness but never to Sarah. Joseph especially felt a deep sadness, and sometimes anger, that Claude had not become absorbed into the family after such promising beginnings. His wife Mireille was resigned, as were most of the family, to an understanding that Claude's tragic childhood accounted for his reserve. After all, he was always there for family occasions and sometimes cooked for them. 'Probably so that he can spend most time in the kitchen and not with the rest of us,' Joseph would argue in one of his angry, unforgiving moments. They all talked, conjectured, sometimes argued and always agreed that he was 'troubled', that they shouldn't bother Sarah with their worries and that she coped admirably and had her daughter and her work to see to. Sophie frequently wore the 'I told you so' expression masking the heartache she had for her granddaughter. Joseph, who had enthusiastically encouraged this match, resolved to tackle Claude one day before long since no-one else was prepared to do so, least of all Sarah. As far as he knew. And Naomi was beginning to sense there was something not quite right. Joseph listened to his beloved

Naomi. 'He never seems really interested in me, uncle Joseph. OK he asks me how school is and all that stuff. But I hardly see him and we never go out. We hardly ever eat together and it's not normal. All my friends see their dads. And go to parks and have picnics and holidays and things. He forgot my birthday.' Joseph was as reassuring as he could be towards his great niece: how difficult it was that papa had to work evenings and weekends, how busy and tired he was, how he really loved her and how she mustn't worry, everything was fine . . . . Joseph always managed to comfort her in spite of feeling angry and hypocritical.

Sarah stayed silent and immersed herself in her work and her daughter's early teenage years. Naomi's fourteenth birthday was a landmark. It coincided with a rare occurrence of a night off for Claude, and Sarah decided to make yet another attempt to have the three of them round the table for a birthday supper; a normal family, except Claude would be distracted, feign a bit of interest and leave the table as soon as it was polite to do so. That was the pattern; quiet, polite, no confrontations, most of the chat between Naomi and her mother. And lovely food. Sarah, with help from her daughter, had prepared a tomato and basil salad and a spicy Moroccan lamb tagine; Claude was particularly fond of North African cuisine. Not that he'd eat much. Sarah wondered why she bothered but knew it was for Naomi, trying to behave like a normal family for her. Although, growing up, Naomi was becoming more aware that things were very far from normal. Half way through the tagine Naomi blurted out, 'Why are we pretending to be like Happy Families? You're not like other dads. My friends DO things with their dads. And they go to places, all the family. My friend Becky went to Alton Towers last Sunday. You won't even know what that is!' Sarah was amazed to see how bitter Naomi was.

'I can't imagine you taking me there and having loads of fun. You just don't do fun!' Sarah held her tongue. 'You don't even care about how I'm getting on at school. You never ask me. All you ever say is 'Naomi, I can see you are fine'—or some such rubbish. Well I'm NOT fine—because I've got a dad who takes no notice of me and spends forever mumbling in the front room. And, you know what? I'm sick of mum making excuses for you. 'He's so busy at the restaurant, he really loves you.' Oh yeah? 'He doesn't have time the that other dads have.''

'Well, that's true,' Claude said, quite unruffled by Naomi's outburst. 'I have an unusual job. I need to work for many hours at unsociable times.' Claude was bored with this talk, excused himself and left the table. The two sat looking at each other, both relieved that feelings were out in the open and both agreeing that, as Naomi put it, he was not right in the head.

The family, not knowing the extent of Claude's derangement, tolerated his aloofness; if Sarah and Naomi were coping they wouldn't interfere, simply be there for them and mutter amongst themselves about Claude's strange behaviour, not at all like a father or husband should be, but at least he provides for them and is never impolite. There were times of deep frustration for Sarah, a longing to be able to talk to someone about Claude's behaviour. Members of the family had tentatively asked if 'everything was alright'. But it was impossible for Sarah to reveal to anyone the full extent of Claude's condition. She wondered if she was ashamed of their marriage not being a success, or was she just not close enough to anyone to disclose intimate details, the bizarre nature of their relationship. Whatever the reason she couldn't bring herself to confide in anyone.

There were times when she was ready to give up, to move out with Naomi, or find Claude a flat; anything to change the situation. Claude seemed worse as time went on, his mumblings and his disregard progressing. Somehow he still managed to present a semblance of reasonable though somewhat robotic social behaviour. He and Sarah scarcely spoke about anything significant and simply got on with separate lives.

Sarah was proud of Naomi's A level results and her acceptance at the LSE. And she was relieved for her daughter; she could now get away from this unnatural way of life and live in a more wholesome milieu. Naomi had grown to accept the strangeness of her father, to 'let him get on with it' and enjoy the love and attention of the rest of her family. What worried Sarah was that she knew she was losing a large part of her which enabled her to tolerate her lot. It was at this time that Harriet blazoned into her life

Chapter 10

SARAH HAD MET HARRIET ON a busy commuter train going out of the centre of Manchester. She never read on the train returning home from the High School in the city preferring to watch her fellow travellers, their telling postures and expressions, their chosen clothing, their reading material; and guess at what they might be, their provenance and where they might be going and to whom. She watched an elderly lady struggle to the seat opposite her carrying an open topped wicker shopping basket, the kind one buys on markets, and settle her frail frame as neatly as a perched bird. The elderly lady scarcely so much as glanced at the navy-blue suited middle-aged man beside her reading his Times, nor even at Sarah opposite and the woman next to Sarah, placing her basket in the aisle, tucking it into the side of her seat. Sarah had been peripherally observing the woman sitting next to her: in her forties, smartly dressed in a black trouser suit, cropped dark hair, sharp fine features, tall and slim, thin really, well manicured, ringless, watchless. She could not see if she was wearing other jewellery but just knew she would be discreetly made up. There was a faint waft of light expensive perfume. Her long thin hands rested on a slim leather document case. She was not reading; perhaps inventing, like Sarah.

'I wonder if she's summing me up,' Sarah mused: beige raincoat, black curly hair, unruly, the morning make-up now tired, small hands with neatly cropped nails resting on a well-used leather brief case, an undistinguished, ordinary woman on her way to cook supper for an ordinary family, to chat about the day's ordinary doings. She would soon know how wrong she had been about her neighbour's thoughts and thought about about how habitual her self-effacement had become. She thought she may grow her nails, wear her smart navy coat, re-do her make-up in the lunch break, sit up straighter.... and oh hell, who cares? Maybe her attractive neighbour was a high-powered PA, a solicitor, a financial advisor; certainly a power-dressed woman of the world; deep in thought about contracts, a divorce case or a pension fund. A lover waiting for her? Or returning to a solitary evening? Sarah continued to muse. Perhaps the elderly lady opposite was a retired teacher who had enjoyed a day out shopping in town, now returning, wearied, to her retired bank manager husband for a quiet evening, a glass of sherry, a simple supper and a little television. 'I don't know why I always make people rather dull,' Sarah thought. 'Perhaps it makes me feel safe, no surprises, just as expected. Perhaps I'm envious of 'normal' lives.'

The train had moved out of the station and the frail old lady reached down to her basket, pulled out her lap-top, then expertly logged on, answered her mobile phone in a crisp voice of authority. 'Yes I'll be in Edinburgh at 8.30, time to eat and discuss the opening of the conference. Usual place. Ciaou!' And continued tapping with enviable dexterity, oblivious of the stir she had caused the two women opposite and the pin-stripe man with the Times.

'So much for assumptions,' Sarah thought, amused and slightly ashamed. 'Now I wonder if this woman next to me is a brothel keeper or a cross dresser.' Half an hour later most passengers got off with intent, to find their familiar niches. The elderly lady moved down the carriage to now empty seats where she had more space. Sarah and her neighbour exchanged brief, complicit smiles.

'You never can tell!' A soft, deep voice.

'No, indeed,' Sarah replied. 'I had her type-cast quite differently.'

'Me too. It doesn't do to stereotype. So how did you sum me up?' the woman asked, 'out of the corner of your eye?'

Sarah was embarrassed and shocked by the boldness of the question from a complete stranger.

'We do it all the time, don't we?' the stranger continued. 'It makes us feel safe, thinking we can predict, pigeon-hole. We're mostly wrong, though that doesn't stop us.'

'No,' Sarah agreed. 'But it's only occasionally we get such a startling contradiction. Nothing's what it seems.' Sarah was a bit ashamed of her platitude. She would never let her students get away with that.

'We created an illusion.' The woman gave a brief laugh and continued. 'Sometimes it's amusing like our elderly techno whiz-kid opposite. And sometimes not so.'

'Yes, I agree,' Sarah added lamely. It seemed like the end of the conversation, both women lost in the thoughts it had led to. Sarah dwelt on the dénouement of her relationship with Claude; more like a drip drip drip contradiction of her assumptions than a startling revelation. And wondered how wrong she may be even about herself.

Two stops later after an interval of slight tension, the woman stood up.

'Excuse me, this is my stop.' Sarah stepped into the aisle and watched her neighbour reach up to the locker above and take down her violin case. 'Were you right?' she asked. 'I make music. My name's Harriet.'

'No, I wasn't. I'm Sarah.' Now, looking straight at Harriet, Sarah saw she was a little older than she had first thought—a few soft wrinkles around the eyes and some streaks of grey in her dark hair; softer than she had imagined.

'I'll be playing at the university next Saturday—I'm one of the quartet in residence there. Perhaps you'd like to come? We're doing the Dvorak quartet in G.' Sarah was astonished by the invitation and knew instantly she would go.

'Thank-you,' she replied. 'And what did you assume about me?' Harriet made ready to get off the train, slinging her case on her back.

'I think you'll love the Dvorak.'

It had been an extraordinary encounter and Sarah felt strangely attracted to this cool yet intimate woman. She was drawn to her, even after such a short encounter. She was at once nervous and excited by the thought of meeting her again, nearly sure Harriet would not remember.

'Have I just been picked up?' she wondered. 'Me? And by a woman?'

The players gathered up their music and instruments after the enthusiastic applause. Sarah walked up to Harriet fearing she was making a fool of herself.

'You won't remember me but . . . .'

'Yes, I remember you well, Sarah.' Sarah was nervous. The woman had been on her mind all week, intruding, welcomed, pushed away, disturbing. Watching her play had increased her fascination. The music was wonderful, made more so by the utter aesthetic absorption of the quartet. The music and the players had seemed to be one.

'You play so beautifully, so skilfully and with such passion.' They stood in the rapidly empty auditorium.

'Would you like a drink at my usual pub? It's just round the corner.'

'Yes, I'd love that.' Sarah had a distinct feeling that she was on a date.

They talked for a few amusing minutes about how they had met and then Harriet said, 'Going back to your compliment, it's all very artful, you know.' She talks rather quickly, strongly with a light mancunian accent. 'Playing with passion is a skill. I know many musicians who don't know what passion *in life* is about. I tell you, there are total shits who play sublimely. And compose sublimely. And, you know, what makes it odd is that there is complete control. We're control freaks. There has to be control. D'you think that Callas singing Tosca really felt those things she was singing about? Of course not. She knew what she was meant to be expressing and did it supremely well; love, hate, burning passion, revenge, and her technique enabled her to deliver. That's all that matters, understanding the intentions of the composer, getting under his or her skin and using one's technique to transmit such emotions. There has to be a degree of cool calculation. I hope I haven't spoilt it for you.'

'It does sound rather cynical.' From the way Harriet spoke, quickly almost urgently, it was as though thoughts came to her too rapidly to express them.

'No, it isn't. You see, the more you're in control the more likely you are to have the experience of being, so to speak, at one with the music—when you and the sound are indivisible. It's sublime in the sense that the logical controlling part of you gets on with the job and then there's the space for that sense that you and the music are the same thing. I haven't the words to explain the experience. When I try to describe it the words seem to distance me from it. Not only do we not have words to describe this sense of one-ness, when we try to express it it sounds trite. It diminishes the experience.'

'I have sometimes felt at one as a listener,' Sarah replied. 'Once, I always wanted to read the programme notes and know about the composer and his historical context. I wondered if a musical experience was enhanced by understanding the form in which it's written and the way the material was used, and even knowing about the trials and tribulations of the composer. Or—just the opposite—knowing nothing and just allowing in the sounds you're hearing. It's by doing just that that I first became lost in the sound.'

'Or found,' Harriet added. 'It's an inexplicable joy and revelation.'

'How d'you mean, revelation?' Sarah asked.

'Well, there's an amazing part of ourselves that we're rarely in touch with and has nothing to do with language and intellect. It's all to do with our senses. Language is a kind of meta-system to the senses, superimposed on them and all too often too dominant in our lives.'

'Yes! That's what I want,' Sarah exclaimed. 'I want more and more sublime moments in my life!'

'Me too. You know, you are the most important in this musical enterprise. Composers and those who interpret the work need to know about form and harmony and many other technical and historical aspects of a work. And need to develop their skills with devotion. You, for whom the work is written, will know about its form and harmony without having to 'know' it. That's the point. The composer's and player's work should never appear like work to the listener. Ultimately it's for the audience. The means are towards that end, that indescribable experience you've had. The work of the composer, and us, the interpreters, is to achieve that end. And of course we the craftsmen have our sublime moments too. That's the bonus on top of our skills. I guess your and my sublime moments are very similar.'

The two women left the pub to go their separate ways home, arranged the next meeting and kissed on both cheeks.

Harriet had sensed a sadness about this attractive woman who had sat next to her on the train. She had watched her getting on, tall, slim, a mass of dark curly hair, rather wistfully beautiful, casually dressed in black trousers and a stylish raincoat. Harriet had been interested and intrigued by her neighbour's sad gracefulness and had wanted to know her better.

They became close friends in the weeks following the concert, Sarah going to most of Harriet's concerts and then eating together afterwards. They knew there was an extraordinary attraction. It took time for Sarah to admit to herself that she was in love with Harriet. 'I've fallen in love,' she told herself. 'A coup de foudre and I'm feeling those feelings I've only imagined I could feel for men. And never did. God, my unconscious mind's spurted out this staggering thing about me. No warning, no pin pricks of innuendo. When she said 'you'll love the Dvorak' she was saying you'll love me. She knew before I did that I could love a woman.'

Something held each of them back from moving to more intimacy. Sarah was afraid of her feelings for this woman and Harriet recognised the fear. Harriet talked freely of her relationships with women and especially of the last one which had ended in tragedy. Her lover, a fellow musician, had committed suicide during another, the last, harrowing period of depression. That was two years ago and Harriet, still grieving, was surprised to find herself drawn to someone else. This beautiful Jewish woman was bringing her and her music to life again. Aware that Sarah was struggling with her feelings, she would be patient. And if Sarah wanted only friendship that would have to be alright.

The two women had started to exchange intimate details of their lives. They were lunching together at Harriet's flat in a smart area of Manchester when Sarah found herself opening up as she never had done with anyone else. Harriet felt flattered to be her confidante and listened attentively, sensing it would be inappropriate to interrupt.

'I didn't know when I married Claude I only had half a person with me. No, not really *with* me. And perhaps only a small fraction of a person, if that. His dreaminess was romantic for a while until I found we had never really been attached by the kind of bond I wanted. I was duped, I'd thought we were in love. He's mostly elsewhere, not with me at all. And now I know where and believe he would prefer to be there permanently.'

Harriet was puzzled but let Sarah go on.

'I've grown tired of his evasions. 'Just dreaming, Sarah. Nothing much. Only remembering.' That's how he is when I try to understand. In the past I've been almost apologetic for bringing him back from his dreams. Note, *almost*. He seems so happy in them. He always returns with signs of reluctance, sadly taciturn, distant. He prefers his life of illusion and I know he's back in his childhood home in Paris. The trauma he's experienced has wiped out his future.' Sarah had already talked about Claude's life before she had met him. 'Now I know I'm on the periphery of his reality, at the edges of his world. I don't make any more attempts—how shall I put it—to penetrate a life shared with ghosts, swarming with images, sounds, aromas, long since gone, yet more real for him than the present. He's a young boy with his happy family and friends where there is no place for me and our daughter. Or anyone in the present. We're the illusions.' The tears flowed now and the sobbing, deep sobbing at last expressing grief and relief. Harriet put her arms round Sarah and waited. After a few minutes Sarah continued.

'Is this OK, Harriet?'

'You don't need to ask that, love.'

'It's just that I've never talked like this before. You don't know what it means to me to be able to bring it all out into the open.' She paused. 'When I look into the dark side of my soul I'm envious of those around me. I'm angry. I feel cheated out of a mother and a father, and now a husband, an absent unfaithful husband. God, I long to be loved wholeheartedly. My darling grandparents, Daniel and Sophie, gone too. They loved each other so much and I'm glad they're not here to see my wretchedness. Sophie knew, I'm certain. You know, quite simply Claude is *very* sick. I think it's called psychotic amnesia. And I'm nearly at the end of my tether.'

'My poor love,' Harriet blurted out. And hugged her more closely. 'I don't know how you've coped all this while. You have to get him to see someone.'

'He refuses to. He doesn't want to be 'cured'. That's the problem. I've offered to find expert help but he just smiles and tells me he's fine and not to worry. I've told him how unhappy I am but it doesn't touch him.' Sarah was silent for a few moments and Harriet left the space there. 'I've never told anyone this but I had an affair with a friend of Jo's, only because I wanted to be treated as real for once; held and made love to, touching and embracing, in the present. I didn't love him. I liked him and needed him just then when I still had a zest for life. Harriet, I've lost my natural joie de vivre. So, to stop myself sinking, I simulate it. But I'm not doing that now. I want to be completely honest with you.' Thinking she had said too much in that sentence Sarah pulled back from Harriet's arms and retreated into her narrative. 'I once heard Claude say, 'You remind me of my sister, Rose.'' Harriet held her hands. 'This was in the early days. I was quite pleased. And then the appalling truth of it all stopped me in my tracks. I put that phrase together with, 'Uncle Joseph is so like my father, even sounds like him.' And put that together with the strange behaviour. Stimuli. That's all we are. It's a simple stimulus-response mechanism. See my face and there's Rose. Look at Joseph and there's papa. He seems to cope with the absence of a stimulus for the response of his mother. Unless I've missed something. Yes, I'm bitter, and sad for him. Sad for myself. All these years of being simply a signal. If he'd said at the start we could have sent him a ton of photographs and recordings of Joseph's voice. There'd have been no need for this charade. I hate him for his morbid deception, his hideous disregard for me and loving ones. At least Naomi's out of it for the time being.' Sarah could feel herself getting hot and her pulse was racing. Harriet was aware of the stress of telling this tale for the first time yet knew it was important to allow her to continue. They held hands in silence and felt close. Sarah calmed. Her voice strengthened. 'I know he's sick, brutally traumatised, monstrous. And well out of reach of rescue. He's a child, vulnerable in a cruel world. He's trapped in a place where he feels safe and can wilfully stop his life from moving on.' Harriet was moved almost to tears imagining Sarah trying to live a life with this crazed being.

'I know the pain and loneliness of not being loved back,' Sarah continued. 'He's alive but dead. I'd feel differently if we'd loved and he'd died, the pain and loneliness with the happiness. He comes back home at night after work, late most nights and tired, and sits in his little sitting room in the dark talking to his parents and his sister. It's harrowing to hear him talking in a childlike voice yet with an adult way of expressing himself. And he has an imaginary person in the room besides his family whom he talks to, describes things, all in a whispered tone of voice. I've heard him describing the shop, the dinner they're having, everything. It's pitiful. I'm usually awake and once assured he's back, I pretend to sleep. You see, Harriet, I care! I always need to know he's back, for God's sake! I hear the talk and I shut it out. I expect he knows I'm not asleep but he never disturbs me. Not even a tender hand on me. Soon after the birth of our daughter, Naomi, Claude lost interest in making love. Not that he was too interested to start with. I have tried to talk about it and to tell him he needs help but I simply can't. It comes out all wrong and then I have to put up with his irritating phrases: 'Don't worry. It'll be fine.' All that kind of thing. Still now after more than twenty years I feel discarded, a wretched reject.'

'You mustn't say that. Sarah, you're a lovely woman and you'll come into your own, I know you will. I'll help you. We'll help each other.'

'You're a love, Harriet. But, you know, I've tried to resist this thought but I feel sure he needs me. There's that irresistible lure of another's need of you.'

'Look, how can you know he needs you?' Harriet asked. 'He seems pretty self sufficient in his dream bubble. It's too big a sacrifice to make. You could tell him to go, find him a flat, explain your feelings to the family. I'm sure they'd understand.'

'Maybe you're right. But something deep down makes me think I have to stick with him. I'm probably deluding myself, maybe it's just that I *want* him to need me. My spirit's closing down. I mostly turn a smiling face to my world which seems to reflect back that it knows my despair. Like a wordless collusion. It's becoming intolerable now, particularly with Naomi who knows there's a serious rift and just keeps telling me to leave him, to split up. And she, too, feels unloved, neglected by him. She's older now and in love but it still matters. Sometimes I wish him dead. He, and we, would be better off. I know it's a shameful idea but it comes to me unbidden. And the shame doesn't allow me to dwell on it. Except on really bad days. Then I dwell relentlessly on a life without him. I can't be locked in much longer. Dear Harriet, you're so patient listening to all this.'

'I want you to live your own life—without him. Or you too will go mad.'

'I know. I think about life without Claude. But as he would say, quoi faire? He is here on earth, physically well, likely to live, I say 'live', into old age. God in heaven, spare me. Of course I don't want him to be ill and suffer pain and die of some horrible disease. But things can't go on as they are. Maybe one day he'll drown in his sorrows, people do.'

Sarah sobbed uncontrollably feeling at the same time a huge sense of relief and warmth towards Harriet who took her into her arms and waited for the crying to subside. She had been allowed to see the secret life of this lovely woman and was moved to silent tears and afraid that Sarah may be the one to drown in sorrow. That afternoon they made love and found themselves in a new world, a world with joy in it.

Sarah decided to stay with Harriet until the following day. She felt she was in an enchanted world and couldn't bear to leave it. At the same time she experienced astonishment, both pleasant and worrying. How had she never know that she was capable of loving a woman; never even thought of it? And would she be courageous enough to be honest? But the present moment overwhelmed her questions. They ate beautiful food for supper, drank white Burgundy, cried tears of joy and forgot about tomorrow. It was the first time Sarah saw love in the eyes of someone looking at her, knew the sweetness of tender gestures and the release in sharing openly.

Harriet had said very little to Sarah about her own life, except her musical life. Now she wanted to share some of her own history. Sarah had asked about her family but had held back her questions once she sensed it was a difficult area. The following day over lunch at the flat Harriet felt a strong need to tell Sarah some of her own background.

'This won't happen to you, dear Sarah, but when I finally told my parents I was gay, that was when I was a music student at the Royal Northern, they told me they wanted nothing more to do with me. I had known I was different from my early teens but I couldn't talk to them then. I didn't really understand it myself. And anyway I anticipated disapproval. And I got it! In no uncertain terms I was a disgrace. They grudgingly agreed to support me financially till I'd finished college. And, you know what? I never saw then again. They've never heard me play as a professional. They never phoned, wrote, nothing.'

'That's terrible, Harriet. I can't believe it.'

'Well, believe it. I don't have any siblings. Of course, it's a bit different now. The climate's more tolerant but there's still a hell of a lot of prejudice out there. You need to know that.'

'Perhaps I just won't tell my family.'

'They'll know. I knew I was gay in my teens but I managed to keep it from them as I didn't have a lover. When I did, she was called Ellen, I wanted to tell the whole world! My snobbish, lower middle class respectable parents couldn't handle it. Bless them, they're both dead now. I don't have any family and wonder sometimes if that's not a blessing.'

'Harriet, I'm so sorry.'

'What for? I'm fine. I'm in love and my music is coming back to life. I'm coming back to life after . . . well, losing my partner. Don't be sorry!'

'It takes courage to be different.'

'Yes, and you have plenty of it. And I have patience. Well anyway as far as you're concerned, my love.'

'It feels like the beginning of a new life. I don't know how I'll cope but I know I will.'

When Sarah returned home that evening her thoughts were chasing around in her mind as she wrote up her journal, long since neglected.

First off, I can't believe I'm in love. I'm in love, and with a woman. I've never felt like this, it's just amazing. I'm alive. I'm gay! A part of me tucked away till now. Something about me that I've never known about. Now I'm wondering how well I know about me in other ways, a thought that makes me at once uneasy and excited. I've always been dismissive of what seem to be New Age-y clichés like self-discovery, self-actualisation but there's a new world to find out about. In sublime moments? Listen, world, I'm alive! Oh God, I can't tell Naomi, James, Joseph, Mireille, Jo—any of them that I'm in love with a woman. OK being 'gay' is more acceptable these days. But me? Other people, fine. But me? And I can't escape from it. I love her. I need her, I want her, her touch, her caress, her abandon, and mine. Joseph would never understand, he'll despise me, and Naomi, her mum a lesbian? No, I can't go on with this—for my family's sake, and friends. I can't go on. Stop. Now. God above, I'm going mad. Did I ever think about what courage it takes people to 'come out'? I don't think I've got the guts for it. Did I say Go Back? Go back, to what I had? Blank out Harriet? No . . . . yes. I'm not thinking straight. Straight or gay, Sarah? I could pretend, put on a 'straight' face and have a gay life in secret. Harriet wouldn't put up with that. Perhaps she would for a while until I eased my family into acceptance. I'm a coward. Sarah Blum, you're a coward and a hypocrite. But I don't want to upset my loved ones. Well maybe they wont be too upset, will they? Whatever. I love her and she loves me and I've never known such love. It's a great gift and I'm going to accept is as gracefully as I can.

Chapter 11

NAOMI WAS ABLE TO SEE more clearly the panorama of her parents' life together now that she had been distanced by her student years in London. She shared life now with James in a small flat on the other side of the city from her family. She was a visitor to her parents' home which altered her perceptions, especially those of her father's grief. The death of her grandparents, Daniel and Sophie, in their nineties, had saddened her deeply when she was a schoolgirl but now she could remember them with pleasure. She had learnt that grief was a normal and acceptable part of life which, in time, would become attenuated. Now Naomi could think of Sophie's sharp-tongued remarks with affection and amusement, knowing her tenderness; of Daniel's gentle slant on everything in spite of the hardships he and his family had known. The two families had been drawn together by their difficulties and their common experiences, and above all by their will to thrive after the Shoah. Her father, as they all knew, had no such will, nor could he have, being encapsulated, it seemed, in a distorted childhood memory. His grief, which he carried around like an impenetrable aura, had become a terrible sickness. Like her mother she had kept her feelings to herself, just occasionally allowing them to spill over to Uncle Joseph. She often wondered why she hadn't told her close friends at school; it seemed to be a mixture of shame and fear of being different, not having a normal relationship with her dad.

It was only after Naomi had become close to James that she felt the urge to *tell*. She had met James in a queue at the Royal Exchange Theatre. They were queueing for tickets for The Crucible. Now, slightly to her embarrassment, Naomi would confess that she simply picked him up. He was tall and broad and blond and solid and cheerful. And she fell for him. She had had a few short affairs, skirmishes she called them, when she always felt as if she were playing some sort of game, doing what one did, the norm. She asked him if he knew Miller's work well and the chatting continued through buying tickets, having coffee in the theatre café and walking to St. Peter's Square to catch a tram. They arranged to meet again at a restaurant in Chinatown and there they were, in love. Naomi moved into James's flat soon after, not the best move to please many in the family circle but her mother had been wholly approving and her father listened to the news with indifference. Naomi at last found herself in a joyful place with a joyful partner.

The time came when her anxiety and bottled up anger spilled out of her and James listened, silently absorbed, not wanting to interrupt and ask questions for fear of stemming the flow. There was plenty of time to ask his questions and express his views later. She had been inclined to be flippant about her father, her way of trying to avoid the pain he had caused, and still did. She knew now she had to tell James.

'Even as a very young child, James, I felt really oppressed by the heavy ambience around the three of us despite the efforts of mum to make our home light and airy. There was pale paintwork everywhere and loads of cheerful fabrics, always a vase of flowers or leafy branches on the table.' Naomi held back the tears and continued fiercely, 'She did her very best, my dear mum. She really schlepped to get him lightened up a bit. She even had the wall between the kitchen and the dining room knocked out to get space and light into that house which you would think had been designed to keep the light out. The 'front room', which was used almost entirely by my father, she'd furnished with lovely floral materials and brightly coloured mats. She'd polished the floorboards and put cream folk-weave curtains up; a bloody miraculous transformation. There were two gorgeous flower prints, one, of those gossamer fritillaries and the other, pale blue campanulas. That lovely little black lead fireplace with inset green mirror tiles. D'you think he appreciates it all, or even notices it? She could have saved herself the trouble.' Naomi continued her mental tour of the house. 'One bedroom was turned into a white bathroom. And, you know, their room is still flimsy and graceful. My room, until I was eighteen, was small, mine, and primrose yellow until the day I demanded dark red everywhere and pinned up posters of Che Guevara.' Naomi laughed at herself and James was transfixed by this extraordinary woman and her story.

'She spared no effort to lift my father's melancholy. It was the only way she knew. Talk seems to separate them. He'll always respond politely and kindly. I can see it irritates mum. Even when she ranted a bit he never shouted back. He never raises his voice, never gets mad. I wish to God he would sometimes, it's just not normal. He's quite simply not real, not there.' James waited, allowing the silence.

'You know he works shifts in the restaurant, sometimes the lunch shift but more often the evening one. You can imagine, he's in great demand, an experienced French chef. The restaurant thrives on his reputation, even changed its name to La Grenouille, can you believe.' She paused. 'I saw very little of him when I was a child. He had no interest in me. He returned more often than not after midnight when he'd sit in that front room for an hour or more with his nightcap, his small cognac. He had a day off every Monday, we had some evenings together when he had his occasional lunch work and always Friday night supper together. Nothing, I mean nothing, was allowed to interfere with this Friday evening ritual. And he does the cooking, the same old meal every Friday; noodle soup, chopped liver, olives, celery, radishes, and a chicken with apple sauce. And he bakes braided bread. I tell you, it sometimes makes me want to throw up. I know now it was what his mother used to cook for feasts, fetes, in Paris. And it was the last dinner prepared by her and left untouched on the table when they were . . . well, you know what happened to them.' James nodded, encouraging her to continue. 'As a youngster I used to get so tired of this ritual, especially the part of it when my father cried quietly and only briefly, when he murmured the little prayer and picked up his glass of red wine. I used to be so embarrassed. Poor James, you've had to put up with Friday nights a couple of times. I can't believe we did it for so long! At least, thank God, he neither cries nor prays now. Who did I just thank?' They smile at each other. 'You know, they are far from being orthodox Jews, my lot, but they do give a nod at some practices, Friday night supper being one, often 'en famille' with dad at the head of the table and great uncle Joseph at the other end. You've been there, it's like a stage set. The family and close friends always gather for the main festivals. Is this all too much for you, love? I am going on a bit. I know you've heard most of it before.'

'Please don't stop, sweet. I want to know everything about you.' Naomi knew he meant it and took up her story again.

'My mother and Jane, Jo's wife, take charge of the arrangements, the shopping and suchlike. And they occasionally do the cooking. Then we do get very *slight* variations on the usual theme. They're both good cooks, confident enough to get on with it without fear of criticism from the professional chef. Dad's always generous with his praise of their cuisine. He often speaks French with his uncle Joseph and aunt Mireille. You've heard them. Mum joins in but her academically learnt French never sounds quite like theirs. Even after all these years the English language has never come easily to dad. He lightens up a bit when he speaks his native tongue. He probably should never have tried to settle here; we're so close to France geographically but culturally so different. And he never goes back. Here he's even more isolated in his grief. Yet sometimes he seems happy in a strange sort of way. I can't quite put my finger on it.' There was a short pause. They were sitting in their small kitchen. James put the kettle on.

'Oh, and those areas of exclusion. Everyone knows the line of demarcation. Any occasional foray into forbidden territory is challenged by silence and a mixed repertoire of facial expressions and body language; you know, tight lips, downward cast eyes, furtive glances particularly towards dad, brow knitting, fingers fiddling with a cup or glass. I've seen it hundreds of times, a kind of general malaise. What steers us back onto safe ground is just a trivial remark, a request made in a jovial voice. A little unnerving when two or more people come to the rescue in unison. Like 'would you pass the wine?' 'I had a customer in today . . . .' 'I don't know what I'm going to do about . . . .' All going off at once. Then there's the nervous laughter and somebody picks up one of the strands. And, hey presto, we've re-established our tacitly agreed boundaries. It's a scream, really, if it weren't so bloody pathetic. I was never sure why in hell there were so many secrets, so many delicate areas, no-go zones. As a kid, I soon learnt the out-of-bounds places and colluded well though not knowing why I did it. Except that it was something about fear of anger, and disapproval and, well, embarrassment. Dad's childhood, the war, Germany, Paris, a long list of taboos. Like negotiating a minefield. I knew certain things. French Mamie and Papi and Rose were no longer with us. They had perished due to the Nazis. English grandfather was never to be mentioned, another tiresome bloody taboo. English grandmother, Queenie, got hit by a bomb. They had all 'left this world' long since. During the war lots of people 'left us.' These trite phrases didn't satisfy my curiosity by any means. I played their games but made up my mind that one day I would dig out their secrets.' Naomi took a deep breath, amazed at her volubility which was releasing and distancing her from the grip of her history. James poured the tea for them without a word.

'D'you know, James, I was sure my father didn't love me. And I still feel the same now. I thought it was my fault my parents were distant from each other and my father rather cold towards me. I know now that's not uncommon. And he seemed to get more and more removed from all those around him. I was so convinced of my culpability that mum had to explain to me that he had never got over the death of his mother, father and sister during the war and that's why he so often seemed sad and distracted. I was nine years old when I heard her explanation and I was mad as hell and not sure why. I'm no less angry now.' Naomi's voice was becoming loud and tearful. 'Even though mum has tried to explain that he's obsessed with his childhood memories. She doesn't go into detail but that's how she sees it.' She hesitated and calmed down a little. 'They don't sit well together, anger and pity.' Naomi didn't want to go further at this point.

This had been the first time she had ever expressed her anger and anxiety. She had told bits of the story, often, in an amusing and ironic way. James knew that the bottle had been uncorked and there was much more to pour out.

He had often talked of his work as a psychologist with children with learning difficulties. It always sounded so challenging to Naomi and worthwhile compared to her own daily grind. She so much wanted that kind of absorption in life. She had decided to finish her training with Phipps and Hargreaves Solicitors and often wondered how she had arrived at this point after a glittering prize at the LSE; the push of the family into a job for life, her need to be safe and secure, a hand-me-down from her family, a strong desire to please her father, her visits to the dourness of her family to find more ways of doing so. Only to be bored rigid at P and H Solicitors and to be increasingly troubled by her parents' lives and the effect on her own.

Naomi's deep unease about her parents became a more frequent part of her life with James.

'I know what my father has been through, James. It was terrible.' He puts down his glass of wine and hugs her. He can see she's had enough. It felt safe to Naomi when his soft blond hair was next to her black frizzy mop. She gently releases herself and takes in his loving expression.

'I can't imagine it,' she goes on. 'He seems so firmly rooted in his past and its injustices he can't move on, move away. Even though he is safe here, his family around him, my mother looking after his every need. For God's sake, how many women would put up with his unremitting melancholy? My dear mum had a bad time, too, you know.'

'Yes love, I know.'

'Her father buggered off during the war leaving my grandma, Queenie, to cope on her own with two young daughters and no money. And then, hell, she was finished off by a fucking bomb and all she was doing was getting her sewing together to take to the air-raid shelter. There wasn't even her body to bury. Christ, James, my mum's suffered too. People suffer all kinds of misfortunes, all kinds of cruelty and injustice, but manage to leave it behind them and get on with it. She still has my grandmother's sewing bag, you know. A little sewing bag, I'm crying over a little sewing bag! I don't know why that makes me cry so much. It chokes me. It had all its bobbins and scissors and needles and a wooden mushroom for darning . . . . imagine that, darning! Oh, God! And I'm scared I caught his melancholy—I get so upset thinking about them all. It's inside me somehow, all that suffering. It just goes on and on . . . .' James cradles her head against his chest.

'You're bound to be affected, that's normal. And it's deep inside. But don't be so hard on your dad, my love. His grief is not just for his immediate loved ones but for six million innocent, undefended members of his great Jewish family.'

'My mum grieves too, you know, and so do I, for our folk. But we can't spend all our days bowed down with memories and hatred and sadness. Why is he breaking up and yet my mum seems to manage? He had such a stable childhood compared with hers. They were a closely knit family with no problems about being Jewish. In fact, celebrated it with relish. They were very much together whereas my lot were all over the place, separate, split up and not wanting to be Jewish, hiding things from each other.'

'People react differently to trauma and it's not always obvious why. Perhaps your mother's life had, in a way, toughened her, given her the experiences which would have prepared her for rough times. And remember she wasn't left alone like Claude was at the end. There was family around to care for her and love her. Claude was hidden in a religious school where he knew no-one and had to be even more distant from his beloved family by taking on a new name, a new identity. All his trauma was buried but nevertheless always there, stored somewhere. And now is manifest in his madness.'

'I always thought a stable secure background was meant to strengthen you against adversity.'

'There's no hard and fast rule. Perhaps it can make one more vulnerable when that stability breaks into pieces. And I'm not saying your mother's experience of childhood hasn't had its effect. I'm sure it has but the effects of trauma take so many forms.' Naomi nods her agreement.

'Well she's not going mad, thank the lord. She's part of a loving, extended family now. But hell, so is he!'

'It doesn't matter to him, my love. He's lost his family, horribly. And has never recovered however much he was cared for by his grandmother, Alice, and Thierry. And then you mother.'

Naomi is still quietly tearful. In the two years they have been together she had never spoken about her father so vehemently. In fact, she had often felt the need to defend him.

'Naomi, I don't think people ever leave their past behind. It accumulates and shapes us.'

'Well, yes. I push bits away. I can hardly bring myself to think of my grandparents and Rose, shaved and naked, dying in a gas chamber, burnt to cinders. Shit! It's too sickening to think about.' The silence in the room weighed on the shoulders of the two of them. 'Sometimes I dream about them, about that last bit. I've read enough to know just what happened to them. But I *can* get on with my life and so can my mum. He owes it to them all to live a full life. He escaped, for God's sake! It's what his parents had planned. I don't know how to lift him out of his history. It's grown inside him like a cancer. Perhaps we do carry all our past experiences inside us but do they need to be so tyrannical? What about change? OK, there are givens, like intelligence, beauty and so on. But misery, melancholy, despair—they're constructions, our constructions so, since we created them, we can change them. Perhaps I mean that the past can show us . . . . inform us about how to live today, tomorrow, in a different way. Oh God, James, I don't know. Sometimes I think he's suicidal, as if he would have preferred to have gone with them; like he's just waiting to see them again. It doesn't seem to occur to him that he spreads his misery over the rest of us. Where is his concern for us, his loving family and friends? We're *alive* and *safe*.'

'Perhaps that's the problem, my love.' James lets go of Naomi and pours a second glass of their favourite Alsace wine.

'James. Why don't you say what you mean?' Her concern and exasperation need a victim. He sits close to her on the little settee.

'Don't be tetchy, lover. I know you're worried. I'm just trying to work things out. I simply mean that he doesn't believe you're safe, that any Jew is ever safe. We know that many parents in the past have tried to conceal their Jewishness from their children to protect them. Just in case. A calculated silence. Your grandmother is a case in point. And your great grandparents. Your mother has told you that your great grandfather, Daniel, used to talk to his apprentice, your uncle Joseph. Told him of their fears and concealment. Told him to keep his head down. They changed later, I know, when they felt safer in their community. So now, you and your generation are proud to be Jews and fearless. You haven't suffered as they did. Perhaps Claude isn't just depressed about the past but about the future, the way history repeats itself in many guises. Maybe he doesn't want to face a future. Your French grandparents had once felt completely safe in France, like you feel now, here.'

'I'm not tetchy, James. I'm just bloody worried about the doom and gloom he spreads about. I really think he'd rather not be here. He's so wrapped up in his past that I wonder if he even thinks about the future.'

'Yes, but escaping from reality is part of his trauma. He's so damaged he's escaped into what he thinks is a safe and loving world.' There's a long pause broken by Naomi.

'OK, so there is still a ton of anti-Semitism around. But we can't live our lives worried sick about what *might* happen. You might as well be dead as live like that. I love him but I have to get away from the atmosphere. Well, I'm not sure if what I feel is love. I feel *something* for him—he is my dad. Mum copes somehow. God knows how she manages to stay so . . . to get so much pleasure from her life. How does she do it?'

'She cares for him in a way but I think she's detached herself from him.'

'What d'you mean, she's detached from him?'

'She knows she can't change him. She's done what she can. She accepts that's the way he is and that's where he is, in a different world that she can't enter. But she's not drawn into his despondent world. All she can do is to care for him and at the same time get on with her life amongst her family and friends. She has good friends, especially Harriet. As you said, your mum's had tragedies, too. She has suffered but she's detached from it so that she can live in the present, in the moment. In this way she's not oppressed by what *may* happen in the future.'

'Well, I'm suffering now. I can't claim anything as dramatic as the Blitz or the Gestapo. But that's where it comes from. An appalling legacy. Like a shadow over all of us. *All* of us. You know, my mother hardly talks about her past. And any allusions to my father's past experience, even the tiniest intimation, throws the family into avoidance mode. I just don't know what the hell it's all about. How you believe in God I don't know. I know you believe in God and I know you believe in a God who is far and away bigger than the petty squabbles and interpretations of Jews, Muslims, Catholics, whatever. But none of it makes any sense to me. It's all problems and pain and misery. And I'm not just talking about our lot.'

'I can see where you're going.' James has that 'let's not get into this again' expression in his voice and on his face, predicting a tearful unresolved outcome. Naomi determinedly continues, raking over old coals.

'How can anyone believe in a God who is at once omnipotent, loving, caring, here for ever and who goes on letting stuff happen? And they're all the same, Jehovah, Christ, Allah. How come eight hundred and seventy million people are starving to death today? How come loads of people are being tortured and abused and exploited? And sometimes by people who call themselves men of God. Remember that story of Beziers—a tiny incident in amongst the madness that was going on around? The Pope sent his army, the so-called Crusaders, to the city around 1100 inhabitants to get rid of the anti-Catholic Cathars, and outside the walls of the city the generals asked the papal Legate, Arnaud, how will we know who is a heretic, a Cathar, amidst our own? And they got the reply 'Kill them all. God knows his own.' I mean, come on, why . . . .'

'Why isn't the right question,' James snapped. They had been in a similar place before and had reached a similar impasse. 'I have said before, Naomi, that 'why' is too big a question for us mortals. Things ARE the way they are. They simply ARE. That's what makes life so exciting. We're not pawns to be pushed around, we don't have our lives mapped out for us on some kind of divine blueprint. Even if we muck it up like your Arnaud chap we have the freedom to do that. And the freedom to do otherwise. I think . . . .'

'If you dare say anything that even *resembles* 'God works in mysterious ways' I'll hit you. I've heard all that free will stuff before.' Exasperation has crept in, rather marched into Naomi's voice and muscles. 'And don't go near that 'There are more things in heaven and earth' malarky. So tell me,' a sneer in the words, in the tilt of the head and the mock pained face, 'what freedom of choice, what excitement for a baby dying of AIDS? For a naked child shoved into a gas chamber? For a person banged up in prison and tortured for his humanitarian commitment? And for a child, my dad, whose parents and family and their love have been snatched away and disposed of for reasons beyond belief or understanding? Tell me again, James, about the joys of free will!' Deep within her tirade they could both hear a note of pleading, raw and passionate.

'I don't know, darling.' James felt her anguish and his own in the pit of his stomach. And makes one last stab at it.

'We're trapped in our rational minds and can't make leaps out of them. We're arrogant enough to think that we can explain everything—if not altogether very satisfactorily *now* but we will be able to in the future when bit by bit more things are known, discovered. It's not like that. The more we know rationally, logically, the less likely we're able to make that quantum leap into knowing that we don't know. The human brain is limited. We're not designed to know everything. It's all too . . . . too big for us.'

'Give me a break, James.' Naomi had calmed into a mood that signified the discussion was over, that they had arrived at the customary full stop, rule off point. She couldn't resist a final quiet ironic enquiry.

'How come you know and I don't?'

'You do know. Last week when we went to hear the Schubert string quintet you told me that you'd been taken into another world, a world beyond language, explanations and reasons. And, you used the words, to a divine place. That's the best I can offer.'

'Yes I did say that, didn't I? And I meant it.' The two of them embraced tearfully in that moment of rapprochement.

'You know, darling James, moving out of that house and going to Uni and then finding you showed me that life can have some lightness. I *can* love living. But dad's part of the family and that means there's always anguish around us. And I just can't take off and leave them to it. It's like there's a magnet that keeps us together. He annoys the shit out of me but he's sick and pitiful. Dad's a constant reminder of stuff we should forget now and move on.'

'We should never forget, Naomi.'

'No, I know. I just don't want it all forever on my bloody doorstep. The one good thing, as far as mum's concerned, is Harriet. She's taken mum out of herself and I can see such a difference in her.'

'Yes I agree. Harriet's drawn your mum into the world of music, of friendship. Having fun and . . . .'

'Having sex.'

James was silent for a moment.

'Naomi, how can you know that?'

'I know what it looks like to be in love. My mum is in love. Probably for the first time in her life. And it's not just the look in her eyes, though that says it all for me. James, she's been on shopping sprees, bought new clothes, new shoes, make-up, perfume. She's got all the CD's the Lindale Quartet ever made. She's had highlights in her hair, she's got brochures for a trip to Verona. And she's stopped putting vases of flowers in dad's sitting room. Don't breathe a word of this to the family. They've welcomed Harriet quite often, as you know, and they're glad for mum that she has such a good friend. Either they don't know or at least not prepared to admit it. And can happily delude themselves that mum and Harriet are just good friends. They can do that unless they're confronted with the facts. And I don't think that'll happen. Or they know and keep schtum.'

'Schtum?'

'Schtum, you schmuck!' They laugh and make love.

Chapter 12

UNCLE JOSEPH HAD BEEN A comfort to Naomi when she was younger, helping her to see that she was in no way responsible for her father's coldness. She wasn't close to aunt Mireille who always seemed to her to be hovering in the background. Sarah had explained to her that, even though Mireille was quiet and diffident, she was uncle Joe's tower of strength behind the scenes. As an adult Naomi knew that her mother, though very fond of Joe, could never have approached him to try to reason with Claude. As she put it 'he was too impulsive and we could never be sure that he wouldn't make things worse.'

Naomi thought it was worth a try to ask Joseph to intervene. Her cousin, Jo, had been quite friendly with Claude in the early days and had tried to get to know him, hoping they may become close. When Naomi spoke to him about her worries he explained that he had been pushed away by Claude and now didn't feel inclined to approach him. He and his wife, Jane, had been bitterly disappointed by his detachment and, given the unhappiness he had caused, wanted nothing to do with him.

Naomi had tried to talk to her father but was frustrated by his bland responses to her questions. Now she knew that her attempts to reason with him were futile. She hadn't pushed her questions as far as she had intended. She was nervous and frightened by her own dark moments. She felt pity and hoped that no-one would ever feel this way about her. Uncle Joseph had known him as a child, was familiar with his life in Paris which now seemed almost unreal to Joseph. He hesitated at first when Naomi approached him. He had watched this family change since Claude arrived. It had been so promising at the outset. Now, people too nervous to mention certain things; then mentioned unwittingly and received into a charged silence. Dear Sarah, always putting on a brave face. Naomi, as a child, bewildered by her father's reserve, still is, and angry now. Claude himself living a shadow of a life and seeming to care little for the effect he has on them all; or probably not even noticing it. And talking to himself more and more as Sarah had confided. 'It was time to have it out,' Joseph reasoned with Mireille, 'to stop trying to protect him. Other people suffered and still manage. There's the family to think of.'

'You know, Joseph, sometimes things are too painful to bear and the only way is escape. That's what Claude has done in his way. He couldn't help himself so we can't blame him. And he won't be able to help himself back into our world. Perhaps we should leave him be. If he gets any worse he'll be hospitalised which would be the best thing for everyone.'

'I can't give him up like that, Mireille. I can't.'

'It's not giving up. He'll never recover, Joseph, you know that.'

'How can you be sure, for heaven's sake?'

'You've seen him, how he's deteriorated, he hardly knows you're there these days. He's never coming back from that. Or should I say 'there', some place where he's not suffering. Why try to bring him back? Wouldn't it be cruel? He doesn't want to be here.'

'People suffer very differently. I have to try. Naomi begged me to see him.' Mireille shook her head slowly. 'I must try, don't you see? We can't know that he won't one day be grateful if we can get him sorted out.' His mind was made up. Mireille could see he had dug his heels in.

He was nervous of the outcome, unsure whether his intervention would be wise, unsure how far he would go. A distance had slowly grown between him and Claude. Indeed, Joseph felt that his nephew preferred not to talk to him as they had done when Claude first came to England. He knew his son, Jo, had had the same treatment. He wondered if Claude blamed him for leaving Paris with Mireille and Jo. They had seemed so close in the early days when Claude first arrived. There was something seriously amiss and he believed he owed it to the family to confront his nephew. Perhaps Mireille was right, he was thinking, and they should leave him be. But he couldn't do that.

Joseph walked straight in through the kitchen and tapped on the sitting room door. He knew that Sarah would be out. He could hear Claude talking quietly. A few silent moments passed before the door was opened. Claude was clearly not pleased to see his uncle and steered him away from the sitting room into the kitchen where they sat opposite each other at the table. Not an auspicious start, Joseph thought, looking straight at Claude's dark, sulky expression.

'I've come to see you to talk to you, Claude. I'm really concerned for you and for Sarah and Naomi. I mean, well, I mean the way you're behaving.' Claude stared at his uncle. Joseph cleared his throat and continued in French.

'We can't go on like this, Claude,' he blurted out.

'Like what, Uncle Joseph?' Claude's tone of innocence angered his uncle who had forgotten his prepared soft opening.

'You must think of the family, Claude, and get on with your life. Your life with them, I mean. Can't you see that?' Joseph's voice was raised. 'You can't go on living in this grey world. It's just not fair to everybody the way you shut yourself off. You don't know how much you upset people, all the family, friends, everyone. Talk to me about it. Please tell me what it's all about! You had a bad time, we know. Now it's time to get over it.' He hadn't meant to crash straight into this.

'There's no need for you to shout,' Claude said quietly. 'And there's no need for people to be upset. Just get on with your lives and I'll get on with mine.' Claude spoke slowly and calmly in contrast to Joseph's outburst. 'You speak of grey worlds. If you really want to know I think that grey is your world. My world is full of vital colours. If you want me to talk I will for a moment and don't ask me again. We know what we human beings are capable of. It just goes to show. No-one can predict how another, or even oneself, will behave in diabolical circumstances. We all, even you, uncle Joseph, have the potential to be unspeakably cruel, capable of irrational and immoral acts. In another time and place those potentials will be massively organised again, sufficiently for another carnage, mark my words. We are forever shocked by what human kind is equal to. We shouldn't be. Why should we be surprised? Brutishness is part of human nature. We don't have a good track record for compassion. Barbarity, we're good at that.'

'But there *is* kindness and altruism.'

'Yes, that's part of human nature too. Submerged under the weight of brutality. You'll see. It's happening all around us. As for us Jews, our history is a rich example of 'man's inhumanity to man'. It'll happen again before long, you'll see.'

'No, Claude, after what happened we have learnt and it won't happen again. Mark my words.' Joseph was agitated in contrast to Claude's cold, incisive response.

'Not in quite the same way, of course. But it will happen. Do you see any kind of justice? Divine providence? Of course not. There is no God, and in the absence of morality there is no justice. Yes, I look sometimes. But now, rarely. It's a torment I quite simply can't bear. I made a decision not to remember, not to recall, all that unravelling exposure of sheer horror and degradation. It's so unbearable I'm hugely successful at replacing those memories with others. It's people like you interfering that bring the horrors to the surface again.'

Claude now seemed oblivious of his uncle's presence. His voice was soft and his gaze distant.

'I am able to retreat from the guilt I feel for being alive into a world I've constructed. Or reconstructed. My memories may not be accurate; such is the nature of memory that it can be fraudulent, but it doesn't matter. I've found a haven, a warm peaceful place. I've taught myself to become more and more absorbed and bewitched. It's where I live. I leave reluctantly to make short appearances, like now. You know, memory is labile. You can mould it to your liking. But lately I've noticed dirty little tricks it plays on me. Memory has its own memories.'

Claude suddenly stared at Joseph as if he had just appeared.

'Good night, Joseph. Thank you for coming,' he said abruptly, in English. Joseph left without a word, and was boiling. It only took a split second to bring back the anguish he had felt when he and Mireille and baby Jo left France. And the blame and shame; his brother David's words: 'Why don't you stay here where you belong? Be courageous, stand up to them for once, whoever they are.' Joseph's life and his brother's death. Claude's life and his family's death. His mind was in flux. He returned home to his anxious wife and burst out:

'We are always striving for some kind of haven and we harbour the illusion of stability and conviction. But the tentacles are still sucking, curling round, squeezing. You know, my story leaving France, the reasons, the courage it took, giving up everything, the future for Jo, has become, in the telling, more and more the tale of a hero. Me, a hero, for God's sake! God forgive me.' A few moments of silence followed and then, quietly, 'I think I've made things worse. I think I've hastened Claude's descent into . . . . well, into what I can only describe as ultimate indifference. I mistakenly thought that if he opened himself up to a close and loving member of his family it would in some way free him, a little at first, from his memories. Now I think I pushed him further into his detachment. I'm an overweening high-handed Jew who still carries phrases from the past in his head: 'impure blood, vermin, waste material to be disposed of, hairy parasites, fat Jews make good soap . . . .'

'*Arrêtes, Joseph! Stop!*' Mireille shouted.

'Those eye witness accounts of the survivors of gratuitous cruelties in that hellish time, the wilful stripping of even the simplest human dignities, the . . . .'

'*Non, Joseph! Don't go on!*' Mireille interrupted. 'Please . . . we've been over it all so often, so many times. And we agreed not to go over it again. Please stop.'

Joseph tries to throw the shroud back over, cover up, make the fastenings secure again.

'Yes, you know, it's the only means I have, I tell you, to live a normal life. Normal, what's normal? I ask myself, is it normal to closet away the diabolical part of our history? But that's what I have to do. It has to be a better way than Claude's. Yes, memory does play its game of 'hide and seek' in all of us. Yet I hear often, 'we must never forget.' We must keep the memories alive to prevent a re-occurrence in another time and place. I wouldn't know how to do that without sinking into a state of perpetual morbidity. Face it, Joseph, old son, you're a coward. I know, I know I am. David implied it.'

'Don't be ridiculous, Joseph,' his wife interrupted. 'David was wrong and he paid for it. Please, don't go on! We did the right thing, or we'd be dead. Including Jo.'

'You know, David, I had my wife and child to consider.' He was explaining yet again to his brother. 'It was the only sensible thing to do, people said so. Now I'm a successful business man, I have my family around me, all safe and spared, alive and well. I leave it to writers, poets, artists, historians, to eternalise the memory of those execrable years; it's not my job. Yes, sometimes I'm tricked into feelings of guilt. I still weep for my family.' He turned to look at Mireille. 'You know that, my love. And all the victims. I think of them every day of my life. And now Claude. The evil's still around. He's just as much a victim, unable to find a way to readjust. His torture is more protracted than that of his parents and Rose. A lingering torment. A lingering torment. Oh God, help him. please, God, help him. Are we Jews eternal victims?'

He fell into silence and Mireille held his hand. She knew there was a bit more to come and let him finish, uninterrupted.

'I have my preoccupation with day-to-day work, the family, pleasure, distractions to shield me. At unexpected moments, especially those moments when I'm at my most self-satisfied, smug, arrogant, the plagued part of myself comes out and I weep, you've seen me, I can't help it. Through the tears I can see I've overlaid the truth with an *almost* impenetrable veneer to protect me, my thoughts about what was done to those who had no escape route, or chose to stand their ground, my sheer terror and cowardice. We create our own reality, you know. And that's what Claude's done.' It's not the first time Joseph has heard impatience in the voice of his wife.

'You did the right thing, Joseph. We'll always grieve about what happened but we can try to live a normal life, the best we can do for all the family, especially the younger ones, and, of course, for all other grieving families. It's the best way we can show our respect for all those who died. There's no question of cowardice for you or Claude. Now I don't think Claude can help himself. He isn't wilfully hurtful, I'm sure. He's simply not with us and I don't think anyone can bring him back. You have done your best. Now let's get on with our lives. I don't feel any guilt or shame. I'm just thankful we got out in time and that we're alive and well. Remember, Joseph, we wouldn't be here now if we hadn't left France. Our darling Jo would be dead. Think of that.'

'You're right, dear Mireille, I know you are. It's just seeing Claude in such a state keeps bringing all the memories flooding back. I think he's a lost soul. And there's nothing we can do to help him.'

'No, there isn't. We could make things worse. Just let him be. I feel sorry for Sarah. She's so patient.'

'I don't think she cares so much now,' Joseph said. 'I wish we'd never invited him to Jo's wedding in the first place. It's my fault, all this.'

'Stop blaming yourself!' Mireille said sharply. 'Don't start being 'victim' again. It doesn't help. Claude is a lost soul and there's nothing we can do for him. It's getting to the point when he'll have to be, well, in a hospital. We need to make sure that Sarah is alright. Staying in Manchester with friends and going to concerts all helps to take her mind off it. We must keep an eye on her.'

'Yes. Naomi sees her every week now. She'll make sure she's alright. But poor Sarah still has to come home to him. She copes so well.'

'We'll pray for her.'

Chapter 13

'That hammering on the front door. Can you hear it?' Claude was talking quietly in his room. 'I can hear it now. You know, the final cadence of my life. Another person walked out of our apartment clutching those oranges, heading for . . . . well, papa called it an adventure. I can see him leaving, a small grey shadow fading fading, fading into nothing. Nothing.

Just listen to us laughing, Rose and I, often at things we don't understand, but we laugh just the same. I tell you, it's such a joyful house where I live. When I get home from school I'll have my petit pain beurré and a piece of dark chocolate which I'll eat too quickly because I'm impatient to get into the shop with papa. Even if he has customers in he always kisses and hugs me. If there's no-one in the shop he'll question me about my day. I answer quickly and automatically; yes, I'm fine, it was a good day. I got seven out of ten for maths and we're doing a project on insects. Papa would say kindly, so what happened to the three points you missed? I would explain that only three of us got seven. I was just waiting to become absorbed in the ticking of the clocks, their cross-rhythms, unequal dynamics, variations of pitch, all vying to be heard. Magical. Can you feel the excitement? I love the way the channels into my senses change involuntarily. Sometimes the big grandfather clock dominates. Or the grandmothers want their say. Sometimes the smallest carriage clock asserts its voice above all of its grown up family. You know, I never know which member of the family will attract my attention when I walk through that door to the shop. Or which one will have flown the nest to be cherished elsewhere. Whoever calls me I go to, talk to and lovingly stroke with my soft duster. I know every clock by heart and always feel a pang when one disappears to sit on a mantelpiece or a table in someone else's home. My loss is always compensated for by the thrill of a new arrival. If only papa didn't have to sell them. My special favourite is the cuckoo clock. I know that one day someone will walk in and buy it but, please God, not yet. Have you ever seen a cuckoo clock? I have asked papa to keep it so I can buy it when I've saved enough. If you can imagine, it's carved in wood and inscribed on its base with Delacretaz, Suisse, 1904. It's a tree with strange birds perched on branches going up to a point like a conifer. The carved cuckoo stands on a little swinging platform just below the top of the tree, ready to sweep forward uttering its two notes and joyfully repeating them four times on the hour and twice on the half hour. Papa has shown me the way the cuckoo's notes come from two small pipes with miniature bellows inside the case.

'Papa, I've finished cleaning the lantern clock. It smells nice. It's smiling at me now, look!' And I can smell what maman is cooking. It's monkfish tails with layered potatoes and sage. She may grill tomatoes and parmesan on top to make it crispy. The shop will be closing in half an hour and we'll have our 'apéro' round the table. I know there are fresh olives. Maman went to the fish market this morning and she always comes back from there with fresh olives. Will they be green or black today? I'll bet with papa. I think black. Rose and I will choose between maman's elderberry wine and tante Esther's limonade. One day, when I'm older I'll have a pastis, a 'cinquante et un' which papa says is plus sec. I suppose maman will have her tiny martini. Dessert is always a surprise, sometimes disappointing when it's fresh fruit and cheese, with a verre de vin rouge for the grownups. One day I'll prefer cheese and a glass of wine to ice cream or sorbet. I remember when we had two peaches, one dried and wrinkly, the other plump and firm. Papa said, 'Now who is the most polite?' I said, 'Rose is,' and took the plump peach. I thought I'd be told off. Papa laughed. 'My little mazik.'

I love closing the shop door to the outside, bolting the locks. Papa always pulls down the shutters to cover the beautiful things in the window. The shutters are too heavy for me yet. This is the best moment of the day for me, a last glance at our gleaming friends, switching off the shop lights and walking through the adjoining door into the dining room. I'll tell you what it's like. It's a small room, just the space for the mahogany table, the straight backed chairs with dark green tapestry seats, a tall sideboard with three large drawers filled with napery and three shelves above for wine glasses of different sizes, champagne flutes, tumblers for water and a ship's decanter with a silver stopper which I have never once seen used. The table's fat legs rest on a long strip of red and blue carpet, fringed at each end. On Fridays, after supper, we go into the sitting room for the remainder of the evening, a cosy room with two stuffed armchairs, both worn on the arms and one with springs sticking out underneath, either side of an enamel stove; our two squidgy pouffes; two tall wood and wicker chairs rest their backs against the wall waiting to be pulled forward for our visitors. I don't really want visitors to come. A bulky beige radio squats on the oak mantelpiece next to the gold and silver carriage clock. Can you imagine it? For a few minutes every evening after supper papa listens to crackling news, even when, apart from Friday nights and Saturdays, it's freezing cold in there. He's always quiet for a while when he returns to the dining room. He never talks about what he's heard. At least not while Rose and I are there. He probably tells maman later. In the comfy sitting room the pine planks stained dark and shiny are uneven to walk on but our feet know the dips and rises. The window, curtained in dark blue, looks out on to the busy street straight into the patisserie-boulangerie whose proximity is so tantalising, such mouth-watering goodies. We're lucky; it's one of the best in our area, the best baguettes for miles around. I can recommend it. Try the chausses.

Would you mind going now? Sorry, but I must go now. Anyway it's bedtime. I leave maman and papa and hear their murmuring voices, comforting, from my tiny bedroom above. I'll soon be back.'

Claude hears the sound of a door opening and is brought back to his sitting room.

'Oh dear. I'm back. Sarah has just returned, intruding. I heard her key in the door. Did you hear it? So bloody trying. It's still a dark place, lighter than it was when we first moved in, thanks to Sarah's deft touch. Are you still here? Sorry, didn't mean to be rude. She won't come into my little sitting room now. It's where I 'rest' before and after a long evening stint in the restaurant. She'll leave me alone. She mostly does now, anyway. She brings me food on a tray. She knows I'm not fully alive except in my 'fantasies' as she calls them. She knows I am more alive in them than I am here. She's right, you know. It has been hard for her. I fell in love with her joyous nature, her easy manner, her mad hair, so like Rose. Well, she *was* Rose for a time. That was what was so marvellous. I had briefly wondered if she, above all, would get me into the present. Not that I wanted that, good grief, no, hell, no. I no longer have those expectations or any such cruel harbingers. There are no such things in my life. Indeed, these people around me are no longer any use to me I now realise. I don't need Sarah now. They don't serve my needs as they once did. In fact, far from bringing my family to me, they interfere with the life which is all I want. They've all started to irritate me with their irrelevance. I mean, really irritate me. I can't get away from them, for Christ sake. I wish I could think of a way of getting away from them. Stupid statements like 'It worries me that you talk to yourself all the time.' 'Who's that person you're forever talking to?' For God's sake, I'm not harming them. I'm not breaking the law. They don't have to stand outside my room and listen! Bloody interfering, that's what they are. And I don't even know you except that you're my friend. And come and go as I say. When I say. OK, OK, I know. It was irresistible and ill-judged of me to marry. But it started me on the route back to my family which is all I want. You see, I can still be in touch with what's going on around me. Nothing and nobody in Marseille had pulled me away from my childhood. I know I'm not normal. I'm not bloody normal! I don't belong here. I perform my duties as a husband, father, breadwinner, friend. Well, to some extent. Time has no meaning for the actor. Are you listening? I cook delicious meals for people. They talk, talk, talk as they fill their mouths, mouths always working, saying nothing, savouring nothing. I could pee in the soup and they wouldn't know. I could leave out the essential rascasse from the bouillabaisse and no-one would notice. I could stop bothering to find rocket leaves to add discreetly to the green salad and it would taste the same. It's tedious and I'm always waiting, getting more and more intolerant. Waiting to take up my real life again, my happy life, and stay there for ever. And ever, ok?

My work done, I down a cognac in one, 'culsec', an old habit, and take a taxi home. Home. I use the word without thought. My home, of course, is Avenue Louis Blanc. No, I should never have married Sarah. She was attracted to my dreaminess at first; called me wistful seeming to like that, attributing my quietness to a lack of ease with the English language. I speak English well now, after twenty-odd years. But I have no interest in this language. I speak my beloved French with my parents and relatives. Sarah knows now where my home is. Distant lives. I am never there with them, Sarah, Naomi, Joseph, the family, the friends. I nod, smile, pepper remarks, feign interest in their doings. They artfully re-route conversations which may lead to my childhood and its environs. I'm glad of that. It's amusing the way they think they're protecting me from the past. They have no idea! I go along with it, their evasions, and I pretend I don't notice. Sometimes I even pretend to look a bit upset when I actually love their 'slips'. I'm a shit really. They comfort me, reminders, you know what I mean? Are you still there? Listen, I'm sorry I asked you to leave.

Sarah and I don't make love anymore. It's been years. A kiss is perfunctory. I never really wanted to anyway. I had a feeling it was incestuous. The moment when she knew I was a child she turned her back, perhaps repulsed by the penetration of a young boy. Now I am free to be that boy again; now I can smile, laugh, watch, listen, talk, eat and drink, touch. My senses are alive. I long for the moments when my daily performance is over and I can go backstage. It's all so bloody annoying to have to stay here. I'm thinking about giving up my acting career. One day the angels will re-integrate me. Hurry up, for pity's sake.

My sister, Rose, has just come home in tears. Papa is in the shop. Maman welcomes her with her casse-croute. Rose pushes it aside and cries into the kitchen table, her arms circled around her head.

'Joupins, maman. What does that mean?' She is older than me, hears disturbing things. 'Sales petits Joupins. Dirty little Yids. Maman, what does that MEAN?' Why doesn't she just ignore them?

'Who said that to you?'

Rose is such a prattler. 'Lots of the kids at school. Even my best friend Marie-Claude told me I was different from the rest of them. She says she'll always be my friend even though I'm a Jew. But her parents don't want me to go to their house anymore. She says they're afraid. What does all that mean, maman? I don't know what I've done wrong!'

I had not heard such things and I was fed up with her for messing up our Friday night. Maman tells her to calm down and that it would all be over and done with, one way or another, before long; that people have different beliefs, religions and were always squabbling about them. It would pass. I tell Rose to shut up. I shut her up. I can choose any day, any time to be here. I'm the Director, you see. I'll blot her snivelling questions. Yet sometimes things do come unasked for. That's started to worry me a bit. But, you know, I am master of my life, pushing out intrusive words and events.

Soon after, we were told not to go to school at all and not to go to the park or swimming pool. These were now out of bounds for Jews. Rose was very upset, always getting upset, but I didn't mind. Instead we went to Monsieur Stainer's house with a few other children for lessons with grownups who had lost their jobs. Of course, I know *now*. I know *now* what it was about. At the time it meant more time at home and in the shop. If only Rose would stop whinging on. My friends stopped coming to see me. And I overheard papa talk about losing the shop. I missed the park. How on earth could we lose the shop? Maman used to say often, 'You can't always have everything you want.' So actually it was fine. Until the hammering. There's this boy, Jean-Pierre Bonnard; pleased I don't actually see him but he's around alright. He's there in the corridors of the school and in the church with the priests and a lot of other boys. I'll ask papa about him. I do know his name. He comes and goes very quickly like I imagine a ghost might. Perhaps I won't bother papa—I don't like the feeling I have when Jean-Pierre Bonnard is floating around. And the others. Alfred Schumacher. My name is ALFRED SCHUMACHER. No, sorry, it's Alain Soler. Father Dominic's a liar! Why do I say that? There's a lot of tangles in my head. Just leave them be, Claude mate. No point in trying to untangle.

Uncle Joseph came to have words with me. He turns up in his immaculate suit, white shirt, always a white shirt, and silk tie. Trying to step up his dignity. He's a tailor, you know. Always suited. The most casual he gets is to take his suit jacket off, remove his cufflinks to turn back his sleeves, and pull down his tie to open the top button of his shirt. And I've only seen that twice. Even at supper he's like a tailor's dummy. His teacher, Sarah's dad, Daniel was just the same. Even had a detachable shirt collar, starched and attached with a stud. Did I say Joseph's concerned for me? He needn't be, I told him so. I now see nothing of papa in him. He's an old man. My attentive listening hat is on as I incline towards him.

'We all love you, Claude, you know that.' I put my armour on, lacking the strength which God is supposed to supply. 'I'll come straight to the point.' Joseph goes on. 'Think about Sarah and Naomi. And get on with your life. You're becoming more and more aloof, as if you're somewhere else. We're all worried about you, Claude. What's happening to you? D'you think you should . . . . see somebody?'

He'd been delegated to approach me. Sarah had long since given up probing. Naomi lacks her mother's resignation, often seeming angry. Has tried to get me to talk. She's too afraid to confront me. Probably senses she won't like what she might hear. It was probably she and her quiet pensive boyfriend who had put Joseph up to this.

'Somebody?'

'Yes, Claude, someone who could help you. We all know it was terrible for you, terrible. But it's a long time ago.' He's getting emotional, pent up. 'You have a good life here, Claude,' he tells me. 'A devoted wife, a beautiful daughter, family and close friends around you. You want for nothing. You owe it to your family to, to . . . stop being so bloody self indulgent!'

Uncle Joseph is overweight. Beads of sweat sprout on his forehead.

'Leave me alone, pretend Englishman,' I didn't say. Mon Dieu, I wish they'd all just let me get on with my life. 'I really don't care what you all think or do.' I didn't say that either. My father's brother went on, evidently now bent on a rehearsed script. I heard some words: Anxious . . . . you owe it to . . . . please . . . . effort . . . . blessings. My face is still appropriately arranged and my phatic responses interspersed with practised ease. It's quite simple. You just match and mirror the sounds and body. He's concerned, I'm concerned. We move together with concerned bodies and sounds. He's angry with me, I'm angry with me. He softens, I soften. Look alike, sound alike.

'We're anxious, my dear nephew,' tending towards me and taking my hands.

'I know, dear uncle Joseph,' leaning towards him and squeezing his hands. It's only what people do all the time, after all. I tell him a few things—I don't remember what. Then I raise my hand to indicate that there is nothing more to be said and he leaves, his duty done. But he looks mad as hell.

I'm getting tired now. All the games. There have to be ends to games. Some win, some lose. Leave me out when the cards are dealt again. I've had enough of all this. It's making my head hurt.

In my seldom here and now periods my heart grieves for freedom ripped from those terrified souls by grasping hands. Must keep the tears back. Those around me, perhaps with the exception of Joseph, take their liberty for granted and complain of difficulties a chained man would rejoice in. I watch them talking, laughing, arguing. Daily I'm thankful for their freedom to decide and I wish they would be so, too. Perhaps that isn't possible in the minds of those who have never known the atrocity of subjugation, the stripping of dignity, the degradation of rape. One can be sympathetic but not *know* in tissue and blood. Must keep the anger down.'

He sits in his armchair, in silence for a while, head bowed.

'I'll tell you something that'll amuse you. I got the sack. La Grenouille takes up valuable time. My routine is: to cook, change my maculate apron for my immaculate apron hanging on the back of the kitchen door, walk among the patrons, ask was it alright 'pour vous?' The owner tells me to use French words amongst my English, only ones they would understand, bien sûr. Like Maurice Chevalier. 'Le porc, as you know, is cooked in a sauce catalane; c'est a dire, avec les oranges de Seville, bitter, you know, and garlic, and tomates. It's a lovely sauce, n'est ce pas? We have to be very careful not to cook the oranges too long or they become too harsh. Vous savez, it's very precise. It's a dish which always takes me back to France. I'm so glad you enjoyed it.' I really don't give a shit. Actually I have a very good English accent. So did Maurice Chevalier. We both do the stereotypical Frenchman rather well. Lately I've been a bit surly with the customers, they're so picky and self-indulgent, eat too much, complain about nothing, treat you like a bloody servant, show off, talk loudly to each other like only the English can, snap their fingers, dress to out-do each other, bejewelled, superior, pigs in a trough, though pigs are nicer.

Saturday came. I'm doing my tour of the tables in my white fancy dress. I flit, laughing inside as I often do in my senseless life. It was such a small thing that set me off, as usual. I've not been too 'comme il faut' at work lately. And it's always something a client says or does. I'm about to change my routine.

'Did you enjoy your boeuf à la Gardiane? It's a dish from Provence, of course. It never tastes the same in Manchester I'm afraid! Dommage.'

'I trust the oysters Mornay were to your liking? Huitres Mornay. So difficult to get the sauce just right, comme il faut. Not a good night for me tonight. So sorry. Cellar V, as you say! You could ask for a refund.'

'Ah. Chateau Rausan Gassis. A wonderful wine. But far too expensive here, especially as it doesn't travel well. As I'm sure you noticed. Tant pis. Too bad.'

'The soup. I know before you tell me. It's not good. Pas bonne. In the kitchen we call a potage de légumes the dustbin! Amusant, eh? Bits of this and bits of that, leftovers.' This particular day when I got the sack it was a couple dining at the window table, the best seats in the house. Big spenders. Champagne aperitif, a beautiful Chablis with the plateau de fruits de mer, Lafitte Rothschild with the T-bone steaks. Bloody noisy, full of themselves, gobbling, sloshing. I watched them through the kitchen hatch. All that careful preparation going into ungrateful gobs. They don't taste the fucking food! The only thing I like about this language is the swearing. I fucked up! That fat craphead and his blousey overweight arsey wife stuffing themselves. I think my English swearing improves, what d'you think?

Chef's tour. Window table. 'Bonjour monsieur/dame. C'était bon?' 'Yes, very good, chef,' big fat bloke says, 'except for the langoustine. Thought they were a little bit on the tasteless side, I must say.' Pompous porker, affecting to be discerning.

'Monsieur, they were evidently too subtle for you. Next time I advise you not to choose . . . '

A hand round my arm steering me off-stage interrupts my performance. Shame. I don't often get to enjoy myself here and now. The taxi is waiting for me as usual. Mr Creighton tells me not to come back and will pay me till the end of the month; and that I was sick and should see somebody. That 'somebody' cropping up again. I'm 'off the rails' and 'have blown it.' True. Blown it away. Willingly. I did enjoy it. I will talk to Sarah in the morning, invent a story. I can't be bothered with reproaches. I know I lie a lot but, you see, it doesn't matter. The time it takes to deal with blame, I don't have.'

Chapter 14

INCREASINGLY SARAH STAYED OVER IN Manchester after work. She always told Claude and prepared food for him and cared less and less about his polite indifference. The family seemed pleased that she had found new friends and interests and they could see changes for the better. Sarah was not about to spill the beans yet.

She and Harriet wrote prolifically to each other when Harriet was on tour. They both found, through the written word, a way of saying things differently, enjoying the pleasure of pausing, reflecting, putting thoughts into new ways, adding details. Their correspondence enhanced their bond, not what they had expected at first when they were separate. It was during one of these separations when Harriet was in Berlin that Sarah was shocked by the sudden appearance of her sister, Josie.

'She arrived quite out of the blue,' Sarah wrote to Harriet. 'She claimed she was visiting an old friend who was ill in hospital. I didn't believe her. In spite of her elegance and self-confidence there was an uneasiness about her. Well, you may say that that would be normal after all these years. But somehow I knew she was here to see me, for whatever reason. I have often had the feeling that it's partly her pride that has kept her away from us for all these years. You know, she set out to prove she didn't need us or want to be a part of the family. I never felt close to her, as you know. I really don't know much about her, except as a very stroppy youngster. We never seemed to be able to play together without arguing and my mother expressed her exasperation frequently by threatening to send us away—God knows what she had in mind—or letting us know that having children was not a good idea. She was so waspish in her misfortune. Yet I never doubted that she loved us—it showed from time to time, strong and passionate. Like when I fell off my bike badly grazing my arms and legs on the gravel and she was so tender, cleaning up the wounds and kissing the tears away. She cried out loud in her sleep when Josie had pneumonia. 'Josie, sweetheart, Josie.' And when we snuggled together in the air-raid shelter. When our neighbours, the Davis family, were bombed out of existence she hugged and kissed us making up for all her sharpness. We became very distant after our mother's death, Josie and I. We had different friends, separate lives. Our grandparents encouraged us, respecting our differences. I think I've told you most of this, dearest Harriet. But it does help me to write some of this stuff down. You are a patient, dear love. I'm trying to get to the bottom of Josie's visit which I'll tell you about in a minute.

Josie and I used to try to keep our spits within the privacy of our shared bedroom. She scarcely concealed her bitterness that I was the so-called clever one, the one people liked, the prettier one of the two, the one with the curly hair. Apart from the curly hair she was mistaken. I never had the courage to speak out as she did, or not do my homework, or stand out in any way—a bit of a creep, really. I never discovered how to counter her jealous outbursts. Now I'm not so sure her anger was the product of jealousy, more likely an expression of her grief.

I was glad to see her go to London and I've seen nothing of her since. Until last week. We all seemed to accept her estrangement. She inhabits a different world, a glamorous world where money and 'street cred' count. I showed you some of the photos of her in magazines advertising perfume and cosmetics. I must say, she still looks stunning in middle age. And tough. A bit over made-up and a rather tight black skirt and top. Red. She caught me in my tracky bottoms and bobbly sweat shirt! Chalk and cheese. Frumpy, or what?

When she arrived on the doorstep she embraced me rather stiffly and I said something unbelievably inane. 'What brings you here?' She told me of this friend who was ill, how well I looked and that she wouldn't intrude for long. I could feel my mouth dry as I made tea in the kitchen and was aware of her eyeing me up and down. I felt such a slouch! We asked each other a few polite questions until I blurted out:

'Josie, *why* did you cut us off so completely? I know you wanted a different life. But for God's sake, you could have kept in touch.' I told her that I had tried for a while to contact her but, getting no response. I reminded her of the letter I had sent to the company she worked for telling her of grandma's death, and soon after, of grandpa's. And that she hadn't bothered to reply let alone come to the funerals. I gave up after a while. I was so angry. Especially for grandma and grandpa—they had been there for us and gave us a home and such love. Until that moment I hadn't realised how angry I was with her, with her indifference.

'I never received the letters,' she said. She had hardly said anything up to this point. It was like talking to a stranger. Yet, underneath all this, I had a strong sense of kinship. Now she started talking and I'll try to remember just what she said as nearly as I can.

'I did feel trapped there,' she said. She speaks with quite a strong London accent. 'But for only one reason. You, gran and grandpa were constant reminders of our mum and I hated you all and myself for being there when she wasn't. Just looking at you now those same emotions are welling up in me.' In that instant I thought of the sewing box.

'I was shit scared when I left,' she went on. Her cockney accent sounded exaggerated. 'Leaving everything familiar, not having a clue about London and trying to look cool about it, you know? I knew I had to do it though. I know now that I had to get away from everything that reminded me of our mum.' She laughed at that. 'Our mum, listen to me! You'd never hear anyone say that in the metrop.'

I remarked trivially, nervous about the direction of the conversation, that she had no trace of a Mancunian accent. It seems that was one of her first goals, to talk like everyone else 'down there'.

'It was quite tricky to pick it up and I still make mistakes like saying 'bath' with a short 'a'. It's 'baaf.''

Pedant that I am I was quick to point out that that wasn't a mistake. She gave me a funny look and said, 'good old Sarah.' I felt like a badly dressed maiden aunt. She talked about her need to toughen up or go under and get trampled on by the 'hard mob.' She explained 'there were girls there, mates, with skin as thick as rhinos, made up to the eyeballs, spiky hair that never moved in the wind even on the back of a motorbike. Quite a few of them were on the game. I might have gone that way if I hadn't met Amos—black guy, and I mean *black*!' She spoke as if she were playing a part. 'We're in different bloody worlds, gel. Sorry about the swearing—I picked up a whole new language at the Young Women's Christian Association! And it wasn't a lot to do with God.' She laughed again and asked if she could smoke. I said yes and marvelled that this worldly-wise, glamorous woman sitting at my table was my sister, that young teenager who'd stomped away from Pendleton Street, Cheetham Hill.

It seems Amos was a gang leader, whatever that means, and a pimp but wouldn't let her do 'the work'. 'He didn't want me sleeping around with any old punter. Lucky escape, really.'

Then she told me that grandpa, yes, Daniel, had sent money for a course at a modelling school! 'He told me not to tell any of you,' she said. 'Especially Sophie who'd have been breast-beating and Oy Oy Oy-ing for weeks on end.'

She went on to say she would never stop grieving for mum and for the wanton destruction all around us by the bloody war. She explained that her life without the reminders was at least tolerable and at best sometimes fun, flippant, hedonistic, a life on the surface—for her part, the way to deal with the loss. There were lonely moments, 'glances inside myself' as she put it which made her want to contact me again and this last time was too much for her.

'I couldn't put off seeing you any longer. Now I've seen you and know that you're getting on with your life I can go back to my life and try to find some happiness. I know that sounds cheesy. I don't expect anything from you. I just wish you happiness. You've got such a bright light in your eyes, Sarah. I'm not angry now I've seen you. I don't even know your family. I can see you're happily married and know you have a daughter. I'm sorry I never got in touch. Maybe we'll send Christmas cards?' She'd shifted into flippancy. 'Oh no, we Jews don't do that. How about cards for Rosh Hashanah?'

Harriet, I simply could not tell her about my travesty of a marriage. Maybe I will one day but she could see I was happy and she wanted to go home with that image. She seemed to have separated me from negative feelings. I couldn't wish for more. I felt such sadness and joy all mixed up. I had thought her proud, ashamed of her family, superficial, thoughtless, hard. Who knows anything? Truth is scarcely there in the words we say to each other, the impressions we give. The mind's always meandering, winding through unimaginably complex circuits while we choose our words and actions for presentation. And then we mix up what we've said and what we've thought and become hard pressed to find the smallest nub of truth.

I do believe Josie's grief has deeply scarred her. She ran away from a pain she couldn't bear. You may find this hard to believe but we held hands across the table and wept quietly. At this point there were no words to put into the space. Then she got up from the table, grabbed her coat and left without another word. I don't think she'll return. And I don't expect any cards. It was a strange, unsettling experience. She's my sister and we shared so much of our early lives. Tragedy affects us so differently.

Speaking of which, Claude is much worse these last few days. He spends most of his time in his room, laughing, talking, arguing and now sometimes shouting, some of this said in his normal voice and some of it with the language and intonation of a child. And it's so strange to hear him shout. I've never heard that before. He never shouts. I'll give you an instance. 'Go away, go away you bastards.' And then followed by a gentle 'Mm. C'est bonne, la soupe de poisson avec des petites crabbes dedans.' And if that's not disturbing enough his delusional dialogues are becoming increasingly spiked with 'get out!'

'Go away!' 'No, no, no!'—something, someone intruding. And now the sobs, the anguish. I've been in and tried to comfort him but he doesn't see me or feel my hand take his. I'm listening to the voice of a lost soul which has been in exile for most of its life, a travesty of life. Dear God, Harriet, it's terrible. He seldom joins me and the family for meals now. I take trays into him, and he returns them to the kitchen, scarcely touched. He hardly speaks to me now. I get the feeling that, when he does acknowledge my presence, I'm just a nuisance, an irritation. As you know I sometimes manage to persuade him to take a walk with me on the edge of Ladybower Dam, the only place, apart from his room, that he is willing to be in. I think the walk is an aide-reverie for him. We hardly exchange a word. He strolls along and smiles and his lips move as if he's talking. He nods and shakes his head as if he's listening. And now he's conspicuously absent from Friday night suppers. They're all very sympathetic but these dinners are now even more awkward than they were when Claude was there. It could be because I don't encourage discussions about his state of mind. They tend to get angry and that upsets me. His absence seems to me to be the cutting of a fragile thread. I apologise for going on at such length. It does help me more than you can know to be able to pour my heart out to you.

Just one little thing, dearest love, before I sign off. I walked along the canal yesterday and came upon a dead blackbird on the towpath. I put my hand on the fractured creature and cried for the loss of its lovely song.

I love you. Sarah.

Chapter 15

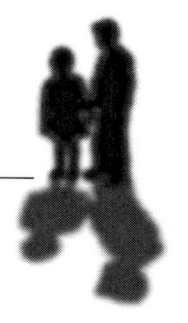

HARRIET KNEW FROM THE MOMENT Sarah entered the bistro that there was something seriously wrong.

'God, you look so down, and anxious. What on earth has happened?' They hugged and sat at the window table Harriet had chosen. She poured two glasses of Muscat sec she had ordered for them. Sarah gulped her wine.

'He's lost his job. And he lied about it.' Harriet foresaw the implications.

'He said the proprietor had found someone else, younger, more sociable with the clients, willing to work longer hours.... nothing was ringing true in my ears. Nothing ever does ring true with Claude.'

'Darling, I'm so sorry. He has no chance now of coming back to the real world.'

'I don't want him back, if he was ever here. I went to see Mr. Creighton, the manager. You know how I like the facts, the truth of the matter. Ironic that I'm living with someone who can't tell fact from fantasy. I've never met him before, his boss. Claude always insisted on keeping his work separate. Well, he turns out to be a plump, fussy little man with a bald head all glassy with sweat. He's all the time leaning to the left when you're talking to him. He nods in a regular rhythm like a basso ostinato accompanying his fluttering fat little hands and the smiling account of Claude's dismissal. D'you get the picture?'

'Very well! If it weren't so awful it would make me laugh.'

'When I talk about Claude it often seems as if I'm telling you about a film I've seen or a book I've read. Anyway, he said, 'He seems to have flipped, Mrs Blum, if you take my meaning and I'm really sorry I had to show him the door.' He has this slimy, unctuous way of speaking.' Sarah skilfully imitated him. 'He's been such a good chef, my dear. Really, really good. And my lads and lasses in the kitchen have learnt such a lot from him, they really have, Mrs. Blum. The young sous-chef will take over now but no-one can match Monsieur Claude's expertise.' He was probably right to dismiss Claude now I know the story but I do wonder how Claude could have worked with such a creepy person. He would keep scrunching his eyes up into what I imagine he thought was a smile. 'He certainly changed things around here for me, Mrs. Blum, I can tell you,' scrunching and simpering again. And then he went on to explain. It seems he had been behaving very strangely for quite some time. And it seems that last Saturday was the final straw. He provoked the manager so much that Mr. Creighton decided that he had to go. I asked him in what way had he been so provocative. He said that he had turned a blind eye many times but now he and his staff were very fed up with how rude and sarcastic he often was with the clients. He had been doing his 'chef's tour' as they call it and virtually telling people they had been ripped off and the dishes were not as they should be. Creighton boasted that he had some VIP diners in that night. 'As I often do, of course.' And added that he thought Claude was not quite right in the head. He had lately refused to do the 'chef's tour' of tables and was becoming more and more uncooperative and ill-mannered. 'I have my standards you understand, Madame. A person in my position has to have standards.' That was his final remark before he turned away from me. I wonder if this guy has a wife and children and how he would be with them.'

'He's probably a tyrant.' Harriet had listened to the story with a mixture of anger, amusement and fear for Sarah. She ordered salmon mousse for both of them.

'So much pretence, Harriet, so many lies in my life. I know we're all pretty clever at deceiving. And the small daily deceptions are as treacherous as the huge ones. Trust is betrayed just the same. But this is a whole *life* lived in lies. What is Claude going to do now? Sit all day in his sitting room? Detach even more from all of us? I'm frightened of what he may become. And what I will do about it; that, mostly. There isn't any point in telling him I know he contrived to get the sack. He hasn't got a conscience, for one thing. He achieved what he wanted and that's all that counts for him. He lied to me, to make it easier for him, that's all. There's no hope for him. Now he has no need to go out of the house. When we do communicate—that's hardly the word—he looks, well, shifty. His eyes dart about and never focus and he says 'yes' and nods a lot, often inappropriately. Quite simply, he's just not present any more. God knows what's going to happen. When we were kids and we did something a bit mad, zany, I remember my grandmother saying, 'Men in white coats will come for you in a white van.' I feel so helpless.' Sarah waited a moment.

'You know, I do wonder, given his stable and loving childhood, well, early childhood, if . . .' Sarah searched for the right words. 'If he wasn't perhaps over-protected. From what I know it was a secure and happy family unit. There were few knocks in his childhood. From that to such a damaging experience, he just wasn't equipped to come through with anything like sanity.'

'Yes, maybe you're right,' Harriet replied. 'Though traditional wisdom might argue that his kind of background *would* equip him with the strength to recover from the trauma, at least to some degree. My feeling is that what tipped him over was having to change his identity. Imagine, given his solid family environment, suddenly having to be someone else, to a point where the fiction becomes 'fact' in your head, where you lose your true identity. And then have to try to reconnect with your real self! No wonder his head's messed up. And all that at such an impressionable age.'

'I think you're right, Harriet. He'll just go deeper and deeper into his fantasy world. Thank God I've got you, Harriet. Hell, I'm really sorry to have gone on and on and never asked you how your rehearsal went this morning. It will be different one day.'

"I know, my love. And the rehearsal was unusually rather tedious, lots of niggling so nothing to tell there. Now let's enjoy the salmon and talk about *our* future.'

It had been a year since they had met on the train, a turning point in their lives. It was difficult for Sarah to grasp that here was a person with no family ties, with a profound dedication to her music and now a love for a woman who was weighed down by the troubles and history of her family. Harriet had been introduced to the family as a friend at a Friday night supper. She had been warmly welcomed by all, even Claude did his charming number. It was agreed that Sarah seemed so much more relaxed since she had become close friends with Harriet; so good for her, someone to take her 'out of herself', the music, going into the city for concerts and meetings with friends, getting away from the strangeness of Claude. As for Harriet, she found the family, all together for Friday evening, noisy, funny, extravert, especially Joseph, affectionate, paying huge attention to the food and wine; and always watchful of Claude. Joseph had made a brief reference to his brother David and his wife Lili. 'Lili indulged David with her braised kidneys, home-made pate de canard, her clafouti . . . he was so well fed he had a tummy to prove it—what we call embonpoint.' The story of David and Lili was received with polite laughter. Swift glances were made towards Claude who stared, unsmiling, into another place. And the conversation moved on, self-consciously. Harriet saw Sarah in a different light, quiet amongst the hubbub, almost subdued, attentive to everyone and at home in her family.

The family gatherings, with all their undertones, made Harriet think of how she had left her family for good when she went to music college. Her sexuality turned her parents irrevocably against her. She admitted to herself that she was envious of the bonds, the support and love in a large family and even the tensions and spits and all. She knew, once she had met all Sarah's family, that it would be unwise for the present for Sarah to be explicit about her relationship. Being a gay woman, in spite of the rejection of her family, and others in her social milieu, was nothing to be secret about, Harriet believed. She was comfortable in her skin. A colleague had once accused her of flaunting her sexuality, an unfair judgement Harriet felt. There was only unhappiness in hiding yet she knew that Sarah wasn't ready to tell her family. Indeed, given her background, Harriet wondered if Sarah would ever reveal that they were more than good friends. Perhaps it would be one of those shared secrets—everyone knows and no-one tells. However it turned out now was not the moment to be open. There was more than enough for the family to deal with given Claude's decline. Harriet loved this woman in a way that she never thought she could again after the death of her partner.

She had now spent several evenings with them all and was always welcomed warmly as Sarah's friend and confidante. Sarah seemed so much more relaxed. The family knew for certain now that Claude was 'disturbed' as they put it, and would never belong to them At least Sarah was able to find some light from under Claude's shadow.

Chapter 16

NOW I DON'T TOUCH THAT world out there any more. Haven't been out there for a while now, have I? I'm master of my world. Master. And I'll soon get rid of you, you interfering, prattling demon, piss off. What's going on here, why am I being bloody interrupted? Don't you forget it, I'm master of this world. Something funny going on. Never happened before. Don't worry Claude, mon brave, you're the master.

Come back, for Chrissake! Just come back! D'you hear me? DO YOU HEAR ME? My pictures, my life under my eyelids keep jumping out of control. Who's cutting and slashing my world? Who's pushing it out, that's what I want to know. D'you hear me? Where are they coming from, all these unbidden pictures, messages, newspaper clips sitting on my screen, bold as bloody brass. Now look, I've seen *that* picture more than once. That bloody picture. Get it off! The poster on the street wall, that monstrous face. Rip it off, the dark swarthy bloody fiend, leering his thick lips at everyone, bulging his black eyes at me, that huge, mais HUGE nose hanging over his wet mouth, JOUPIN DEVIL EXTERMINATE all over it. You know, that's supposed to be a Jew. Do I know a Jew who looks like that? Oy-oy-oy! Do I know a Jew who looks like that? Switch the bloody tele off!

Now he's changed. It's papa! You see? I can change a fiend into a father in a second. I'm a master of transformation. Cabbage into garbure; liver into fois gras; Sarah's love into pity; my torment into pleasure; and the rest of it. I'm in control. *I am in control.* And so here I am, back home again. Everyone nice, smiling, laughing. Maman asking, 'Would you like more soup, mon cher?' 'Non, merci, maman, j'ai plus faim.' Uncle Benjamin will soon be here. A schmooz night tonight. He'll play for us before bedtime. He drinks cognac, Uncle Benjamin. His big, plump hands clump around the little glass. Then they turn into agile maggots jumping and sliding around the strings.

I'm *trying* to listen to the Bach unaccompanied Suite in C major. He'll play just the Bourrée 1 and 11. My favourite Bach. It seems to be fading away. What the hell is going on? God above, it's gone, the music. Shit! Shit! Go away! I don't ask for them to come to the surface. One after the other. And I have to read them, I have to read them.

"He played the violin for the Germans and lived a little longer.

For journeys of many days they were packed so tightly in cattle trucks they could not sit down; until space was made by the dead, removed at each stop.

We will have a thousand year Reich populated by blond blue-eyed Aryans. Everyone blond and blue-eyed. Rid of the pollution of dark eyes and dark skins.

Drancy . . . .

It's chaos, thrusting itself into my world. Chaos. Am I losing my power? Oh God, no! Claude, you're losing your power, mon pôte. I'm losing it. I can't find the right switch; I can't turn onto the right channel. And always sobbing, sobbing, always bloody sobbing, for God's sake! I'm losing it. Feh! You're losing it Claude, old chap.

Un-clench your teeth then you can shout.

'Maman, papa, don't leave me! Rose, I'll never argue with you again. I'll buy the cuckoo clock for you, I'll do my homework on time. You'll be proud of me. I'll wash the dishes. You see if I don't! Just you see! I won't swear ever again. Oh God, come back! Don't leave me again please, please, please. COME BACK! DON'T LEAVE ME AGAIN!'

I'm always sobbing. It's so dark inside this fucking clock. My eyes are focussing on nothing. Now they're flooded with fritillaries and green tiles. I'm not kidding! My ears throb with the cacophony of doors, drawers, doors, drawers, grief. Boum, boum, on and on. Alfred Schumacher is a wet rag doll. A front door slams into my ears again. Will you teach me to play the cello, Uncle Benjamin? Father Dominic is crying in chapel. The clocks have gone mad, ticking and chiming all together. I am Jean-Pierre Bonnard and my parents are in America, they're coming back for me. Please come back. DON'T GET ON THAT TRAIN! The gassing, burning, gassing burning, gassing burning. . . . . a routine. Desensitised souls at their work, that's what they are. Those heaps and heaps . . . . little Rose, where are you? Papa, I don't like this adventure. Naomi is angry. I have a daughter, you know. How can a boy have a daughter? Vautour, le Docteur, Chappelle, l'Ingénieur, Gazelle, Aramis. My name is Jean-Pierre Bonnard. My parents are in America. Thierry is in Marseille. My parents are not in America. This is my dream room. Sarah made it nice. Uncle Joseph came in and talked at me. I told him a thing or two. What did I say? I didn't offer him a cognac. He left and Benjamin came to see me. He loves his cognac, fat fingers cognac. He played. What is there to laugh at? Papa made a big mistake. I couldn't pick up the oranges. Father Michel is dead. Boys, let us pray for him. I couldn't pick up the bloody oranges! What a joke! D'you hear that, papa? I couldn't bend! You didn't think of that did you, when you left me? Did you? Daniel was kind. And Sophie knew, she knew, I saw in her eyes she knew. Died peacefully when they were ready. No Drancy. No trains. No gas. Proper funerals. Daniel was like Father Michel, silvery, gentle. Marseille grandma gave up the struggle. A little bird. A little dead bird.

I'm tired. I'm responsible. I'm guilty.

Now all the pictures are fading, mixing up. All sounds are white noise. The bad and the good entangled.

My screen's gone blank, the sounds gone, nothing there. I've lost it! I've lost it!

I'm so bloody tired.

'Why art Thou so far from helping me, from the words of my groaning?'

I'll go for a walk by the water with papa. Shall we do our usual walk, papa? Please. Now, my friends told me that angels live in the water. Do you believe that, papa?

I'm tired now. Tired.

Chapter 17

SARAH'S LIFE HAD BECOME ONE of sharp contrasts; the magic of being with Harriet, the pleasurable routine of teaching, and the frightening madness of being at home with Claude, the last becoming nearly unbearable. Sometimes, as she walked through the front door after work, he would be talking quietly and other times there would be stark silence. Increasingly often, out of the quiet murmurings, or the silence, would come shouting and cursing in a voice full of anger and anguish. Then it would subside. Sarah's first action as she walked into the house was to turn on the radio. The days had long since gone when she listened at the door to try to make sense of what he was saying or to assess his mood. He had become incoherent and with more and more outbursts. It was getting difficult to time when to take a tray of food into him. Once, she would wait for a silence which she knew would last a while, then tap on the door and walk in. He always looked at her and smiled, sometimes even said 'Hello Sarah, how are you?' He appeared to listen to her attempts to describe the day but his eyes gave away his indifference. He would give bland responses to her enquiries about his day. These days he scarcely left the room and would put the tray on the floor outside his door, sometimes untouched. Now Sarah prepared food and, unless he was shouting, would walk straight in, put the tray on the little table and say hello and smile. Sometimes he smiled back but latterly he would continue to mutter and stare straight ahead. There was no point in making any more appointments for him to 'see someone', Sarah had concluded. She had made several but either he didn't turn up or turned up and put on such a good performance of normality that she was sure the doctor thought she was exaggerating. Sometimes pills were prescribed and never taken.

Sarah arrived home later than usual after a long staff meeting and a delayed train. She walked into the long, narrow hallway, put her bags on the hall table, hung her coat on one of the brass hooks and wondered whether to go and make supper first before saying 'hello' to Claude. Not that he responded these days except very occasionally. It never stopped being strange to come home and know he was there, alone, in his own world, in his sitting room, a deranged human being. She had grown used to evenings alone. She would make a simple supper, an omelette and salad and think about the last and the next meeting with Harriet. Tomorrow evening they would meet at an Indian restaurant after work, a day's rehearsal for Harriet. She'd wear her new jacket with the dark red scarf. She always told Claude of her plans and always left food for him in the fridge. It usually stayed there. He ate so little he was becoming thin and gaunt, looking years older than he was, clothes hanging loosely. His large dark eyes had begun to protrude. And he stared and stared into the distance. He was beginning to look grotesque, his cheeks sinking, pulling his full mouth into a pout, his hair long, his skin taking on a greyish pallor. Oddly he took care over his hygiene and clothes. He was always clean and neat, childhood habits he clung to.

She'd tell him later that she would be staying over tomorrow until the following evening. She knew he wouldn't be listening to her, and if he did, wouldn't remember what she'd said. It made no difference to him. In fact she knew that he found her irritating when she walked into his room. She felt no guilt now about leaving him for a day and a night. Her feelings towards Claude had changed over time, but dramatically since she met Harriet. And not only because of her love for Harriet but because Claude's condition had worsened and she could see now so clearly that this was an extreme effect, utterly damaging, of terrible traumatic experiences. She felt great sadness when she saw him or thought about him. He had never loved her or even cared for her in any significant way, merely and rather cleverly trapping her into his crazed world, using her as a channel to another world. She worried about what would become of him, how would the illness evolve, would they eventually have to put him into a psychiatric hospital. Harriet had helped her to see that there would be an end to the nightmare and in the meantime to find deep compassion for him.

Naomi hardly ever came to the house now. Her father didn't acknowledge her; appeared not even to recognise her. His appearance frightened her. There never had been a place for her in his life. Naomi worried less about her mother since it was clear to her that she had the love and support of Harriet. She and Sarah met every week in town for a lunch or supper and sometimes with Harriet. Aside from the fairly brief 'How's he been this week?' conversation, talked mostly of other things. Sarah had lately talked of his increasing outbursts but, that said, they'd been over all the ground and it was a relief to get away from talk of him.

Sarah poured herself a glass of wine and sat in the kitchen wondering in a desultory way about prawns and pasta or prawns and stir-fry vegetables and that Naomi seemed to know about her relationship with Harriet. She often looked at her mother in a knowing little way when they talked of Harriet and the music. Sarah was sure she knew of the love between them. Should she do her marking this evening or get up early? It suddenly occurred to her that she hadn't heard a sound from Claude's room. Perhaps he's asleep, she thought, or maybe moved on to another, less vocal stage. She stood up, walked quickly, nervously, holding her breath and opened his door. Claude was not there.

'Christ!' Sarah shouted. 'Where the hell is he? He's never done this before. Claude! Are you in the house?' Not a sound. 'Oh, fuck, Claude, don't do this to me!' She ran into every room of the house, glanced at the little garden and rang around the family; to no avail, everyone anxiously offering to help, come round, go and look for him. 'Where would I look for him? He never goes anywhere.' She rang the two local hospitals, ran to the car and drove to the restaurant where he used to work, to a pub nearby where he used to have an occasional drink and then to the police station. No-one knew anything. 'The best thing you can do, Ma'am, is to go home and wait there for news.' When she arrived home she made more phone calls, paced up and down, tearfully talked to Harriet then Naomi. She sat in silence for some time, waiting for him to come through the door, wondering fearfully where he might be.

'Oh, God, he's so vulnerable out there,' she thought. 'He doesn't know his way around, he's naive.' She started talking aloud. 'Why would he go out? He never wanted to go out. He hasn't left the house in a long time. I just don't know what to think. For Christ sake, Claude, get back here!'

There was a knock at the door and Sarah leaped to her feet remembering he probably didn't have a key. The policewoman gently informed her that Claude had been found drowned in Ladybower Dam. She advised her to call a member of the family to come and be with her.

No tears came. Just blankness. Silence. Stillness. Staring. For a long time. Harriet arrived to find her in a numbed state of shock. She stayed with her and the tears and release finally came.

'I can't believe he's gone, Harriet,' Sarah sobbed. 'There's no note, nothing. Just walked out to the dam and . . . .'

'We'll have to wait for the postmortem.'

'I don't need to, Harriet.' She was weeping quietly now. 'You know, I feel an enormous sadness mixed with a great sense of release. It's strange to feel these emotions together so profoundly. I didn't love him. He was, really, a stranger to me. But that doesn't stop me feeling so sad for him. A true part of him lives on in Naomi. I can love him that way.'

'Let me take you back to the flat. I don't want you to stay here. We can do what we have to do tomorrow.'

'Yes. Let's leave here.'

The house and most of its contents were sold very quickly. Sarah knew there was no looking back now, no regrets, no recriminations, and no more yearning to be loved and love. It was a hugely liberating time for her, filling her with excitement but with sorrow around its edges. She wondered if Claude would always be there, around the edges, haunting though not menacing. He was a large part of her history.

The family could not help their relief at the death of Claude. Joseph often reflected on Sophie's words and doubts. She had seen something none of them had seen in those early days. He could almost hear her: 'There, you see, Joseph?' with a shrug of the shoulders and spreading of the hands. Claude had left a world he didn't belong in after the Gestapo raid and Joseph, Mireille and the family were, above all, thankful that he was no longer in torment. And couldn't now blight the lives of others. 'But, you know,' Joseph said to Mireille, 'in some way or another he'll always be around. Perhaps to keep us reminded.'

Sarah and Harriet moved into a large ground floor flat with its own garden in the smart suburbs of Manchester. Some of the family and friends gave thanks for the lovely friend Sarah had found, others rejoiced in Sarah's lover. And Sarah knew a sense of freedom and lightness that she could not remember ever having. The flat had huge windows at the back which opened onto the garden and let vast light into the large living room. 'Room to live,' Sarah thought when she first saw it.

'Harriet, we have to have this place,' she had said, standing by the window looking down the long narrow garden.

'I agree. The light is wonderful and you need it, my love.'

'And you too. Hold my hand. We can grow vegetables right at the bottom there, and maybe make this top end a rose garden. And I'd like a white area like Vita Sackville-West at Sissinghurst. Well, a little bit like it. What d'you think?'

Harriet was scarcely listening watching this beautiful woman emerging from the horror and darkness of so many years. 'It'll be a long time,' she thought, 'before she'll be completely free from this part of her life; indeed, if ever. Perhaps it will always cast a shadow over her. And others.'

They bought the flat and moved in at the first possible moment. They had a joyful weekend buying what they immediately needed. Naomi and James helped them move in, fetch and carry, clean, shop for the weekend's meals. Naomi bought lobster, welsh lamb, fresh vegetables from the farm shop, mangos, her mother's favourite fruit, champagne, white Burgundy, and Rioja. 'Our small token—to wish you great happiness here.'

'You're such loves.' Sarah felt tearful as she stood in the kitchen watching her daughter fill the fridge and thinking, 'I love that girl so much. She'll get over it and be thankful and free.'

'Mum, I can't tell you how—I'm just bursting with joy and relief. It's a new life for you. Go out and have a super hairdo, buy a load of new clothes, sexy undies—oops, did I say sexy undies? Come on mum, I know you're in love and it's fabulous. Chuffin' bloody wonderful!'

Mother and daughter embraced each other and shed tears while James and Harriet stood in the kitchen doorway loving this beautiful moment.

Harriet and Sarah walked the length of the garden making their plans; a little herb patch here, a colourful herbaceous border along the brick wall separating them from next door's long garden, a weeping birch in one corner, clematis against the house wall. The evening dinner was a celebration of their new home together, their new lives, and the meal was served on their new white porcelain dinner service from John Lewis. Sarah prepared fish soup and roast lamb with fresh peas and mint, and wondered if she'd ever eat chicken and braided bread again.

'He couldn't swim, you know,' she said. 'He was afraid of water.'

Harriet waited.

'He'd never done that walk alone.' They sipped their champagne from gleaming new flutes.

'I think,' Sarah continued, 'we'll get a lovely buttoned chesterfield for in here. What d'you think?'

'Great idea. And how about voile curtains for these big windows? Purple.'

'Purple? Well, OK. Purple. Yes, purple! And a really fussy chandelier.'

'I love you and you're safe.'

'I know, sweetheart, and I've never felt so wonderful in my life.'

There was a long pause as they held hands across the table and smiled at each other.

'Harriet, what does 'misadventure' mean exactly?'

'I think it means an accident but with no suspicious circumstances.'

They hadn't spoken about this. Harriet knew that Sarah believed Claude had committed suicide but she was unable to bring the issue out into the open. After a few moments Sarah continued.

'They said after the postmortem that he'd had a heart attack. How could they know whether that was before or after he went into the water? *I* know what he did and I'm deeply thankful, Harriet. Alright, I know he did it for himself and not for me, or anyone. He wasn't able to care for even those closest to him. He simply couldn't. We weren't in his world. He did what he did simply to be re-united with his family. And I'm glad he did it, for his own sake.'

'Yes, and it was for everyone, even though he didn't know that.'

'It'll always be with me, you know, the tragedy of it. And maybe that's how it should be. I hope that won't spoil things for you.'

'It's part of you. How could it spoil anything for me?'

'It'll be with all of us who were around him. But we can still live joyfully, can't we? We have to preserve the memory of what happened. Those of us directly affected carry the heaviest load. I nearly said 'burden' but, well, it's not a burden. It was all too much for Claude to bear. You know, Harriet, now I don't feel any blame, resentment, anger, any of that. Of course he wasn't gassed but they took his life just the same, he was a victim of the Holocaust just the same. And so am I and millions of others. I hope the next generation suffer less. I remember reading somewhere that history accumulates inside us through generations. Dearest Naomi.' Their thoughts silenced them. Sarah was the first to speak.

'I like the idea of purple curtains. And the showy chandelier. Oh God, it's lovely here. I just love it. Am I dreaming?'

'It is like a dream. Remember the elderly lady with her lap top on the train? And the first time you came to a concert? The Dvorak. It does all seem a bit dreamlike. But it's real and we're going for it—fun, tons of fun, music, lobster, you name it.'

'I will—we're going to see the magic mountain, Canigou. It's in the Pyrenees, the Mediterranean end. I fell in love with it when I was a student but have never been back since. I've been waiting for the right time. And this is it.'

'It sounds wonderful.'

Chapter 18

NAOMI ASKED HER MOTHER AND Harriet if she and James might invite family and close friends to their flat for a dinner, their own place being much too small. The date and time were agreed on and Sarah asked, 'Is it for anything in particular or just a get-together?'

'Well, it's a month now since dad died so I wanted to celebrate new beginnings. Especially for you and Harriet. And for Jo and Jane and their new baby. And for all of us; free now that dad has gone. Oh God, that sounds awful. I didn't mean it to come out like that. But you know what I mean.'

'Of course I do, darling. I want everyone to know that I don't want Claude's name to be avoided. He's been part of all our lives and, sick though he was, mention of him is never to be taboo. I trust we'll all honour his memory, the memory of his suffering.'

'I know we will.'

'Now, the dinner is a lovely idea and I'll help you.'

'No mum. I want to do this myself. You and Harriet go out for the afternoon.'

The Friday night suppers had ceased. The old patterns were disappearing much to the relief of all. The family and friends had wept for Claude at the funeral, had wished him and themselves peace, and had experienced deep compassion for him. Emotions had run high, and mixed; relief at Claude's release from his ghosts, sadness for a lost child, gladness for Sarah's freedom and future. And bewilderment at why and how this ever happened. Mireille was worried that Joseph seemed unable lately to control his tears. He would be better after the funeral, she was sure.

It was just after the funeral that Naomi had made the decision to bring everyone together, at a later date, to enjoy a happy time and look forward. She and James decided on a menu of fresh salmon with fennel sauce followed by roast beef and Yorkshire pudding. James would bake meringues for dessert with Chantilly cream. No candles. Not a chicken leg or olive in sight.

It was a lovely sunny evening and the guests enjoyed their aperitifs in the garden in a relaxed and warm atmosphere. The supper was splendid, everyone in good heart, even Joseph rising to the spirit of the occasion. After dessert Naomi stood up, beamed at everyone and announced, 'We're going to have a baby!' The room erupted with joyful sounds, applause, tears, re-filled glasses, hugs. Joseph, unable to break the habit, stood up to make many effulgent toasts about the future, love, babies, remembering, new beginnings.

'A new generation,' Harriet whispered to Sarah. 'Let's drink to the baby's grandmother.'

'Yes. And grandfather.'

About the Author

GAYNOR GABRIEL IS A PSYCHOLOGIST who has lived in the French Pyrenees for many years where she was writing and teaching. She has now moved back to the UK, to a village on the edge of the Peak District, near to her family.'